A WORLD FULL OF

BEAUTIFUL

PEOPLE

Mom, this one's for you.

Love is a Journey.

A WORLD FULL OF BEAUTIFUL PEOPLE

BRITIAN BELL

ONE

F lying through the forests of Kawaii at speeds of 60 miles per hour would elevate anyone's heart rate. Adan is no exception, as he screams at the top of his lungs during his zip-line through the trees. The leaves are so close they brush his skin. For the moment, he is carefree, until the zip-line wire breaks, and he crashes to the ground at a startling speed. His daydream is abruptly ended by the sound of a new email, an autogenerated update of no significance. *Figures.*

Scrolling through listing after listing of all-inclusive vacation stays in Hawaii, believe it or not, does become monotonous. Adan would prefer to be anywhere other than at work; a tedious job would be a kind description of the eight hours a day he spends at the office. Between 2 p.m. and 3 p.m. most days, Adan is usually searching for a vacation getaway of at least two weeks. Of course, he never finds anything he is willing to pay to reserve at the time, but the search itself does help remove him from the office for a short time.

Adan is rarely satisfied in the present; he longs for something more fulfilling. Unable to decide whether it is an experience or something else he desires, he closes his laptop, packs his bag, and leaves work at 4 p.m.—an hour early.

Leaving work early is not uncommon for Adan; he has no guilt over it, though, since he works through his lunch regularly, at least on the days he wants to leave work before 5 p.m. Today has the potential to disturb the boredom that a long day at work gifts, though—dinner at Grandma's! Not an overly exciting evening, but certainly better than sitting at home indulging in a TV show. His preference for conversation makes Adan unique, but it also makes him a boring 20-year-old.

Adan has a full-time job, is taking college classes part-time, attends church regularly, and has no friends his own age. And the friends he does have, he doesn't see or talk to frequently, which makes him question whether he actually has these friends; this, he says, "is the definition of a dull and uninteresting person." His grandma, however, has a different opinion.

Adan pulls into his grandma's driveway but has to park more in the yard than the driveway since the rest of his family has already arrived. As he makes his way to the entrance of his grandparents' cozy, rustic log home, he takes pleasure in the authentic Italian smell of the food his grandma has prepared.

Lasagna with garlic bread is my favorite!

Pulling the door closed behind him, he can hear his family's chatter bounce throughout the house. As always, politics and news are on the discussion agenda tonight. *Predictable as the sunrise.*

"Hey, Adan," Grandma says as he walks into view.

"Hi, Grandma. How was your day?" he asks.

"My day was fantastic, Adan!" she exclaims. "Do you know why?" She is standing at the counter chopping the last of an onion to finish putting together a salad.

"What made today fantastic, Grandma?" he asks.

"I am spending my evening with the people I love dearly. What could be more fantastic than that?" she says.

Love is something Adan has always known. He has been clothed with love from a family who not only says, "I love you," but expresses it through action. Grandma is the one who deserves the credit. She is the one who taught the whole family what love is.

"I see, and you make my day fantastic too, Grandma," he says.

"That isn't a compelling tone, but I'll still take it."

At the dinner table, Ashby complains about Adan taking his seat. "This seat was open!" Adan shouts.

"I was using the bathroom, duh. That doesn't mean you can take my spot," Ashby reminds him.

It's a stupid chair; just shut up.

Younger siblings are a blessing and a curse; Adan is becoming impatient as he waits for Ashby to mature, so hopefully, they can be friends instead of what can be best described as "bickering brothers."

After Ashby guilts Adan into moving to a different chair, Adan finds a seat next to his mom— his favorite person in the world. Renee is a strong and beautiful woman whose character is shown in her and her three sons, Adan, Ashby, and Odell, the oldest.

Mom looks at Adan with her emerald, green eyes and lovingly says, "Run your hand along the side of your head; you have a few hairs sticking out."

"Thanks, Mom." He rolls his eyes. "I hope your day was good, too."

"It was." She chuckles. "No blood today at the hospital!"

"Definitely a good thing!" Adan exclaims. "A slow day for you means few sick or injured people."

"Exactly," she says.

After finishing some small talk with his mom, Adan listens in on the conversation between his dad and grandpa about how democratic presidents suck. That is one thing about living in the central United States; everyone has a strong opinion about almost everything, political leaders included.

Adan was interested in politics as a teenager. Now that he has matured and entered the workforce, he has no time or energy to discuss such meaningless topics. He likes discussing subjects such as psychology or the stock market. He'll even gossip about family and neighbors. Adan isn't proud to admit the latter, but that doesn't make it any less true.

"Adan, what did you learn today?" Grandpa asks loudly.

"Well, Grandpa, not a whole lot," Adan responds. "Work is uneventful right now, as usual."

"Sounds like the place to be," Grandpa jokes.

Adan's grandpa is a gruff but lovable older man, easy to talk to and faithful to his family.

Adan and his dad never greet each other; there is no need, a conversation can start from thin air between them. "I saw you on your way to work today. Ten minutes after 8 a.m. You were late," his dad says.

Adan nods his head, changing the subject. "How is Uncle Alden doing?" Dad spends at least half the day every Tuesday visiting with his brother.

"He's doing fine, as sour and grouchy as ever."

Uncle Alden rarely comes around the rest of the family. Dad is one of the only members of the family he will talk to and the only one he will allow in his apartment. A life spent chasing the next high ironically leads to the deepest low. Adan has never had any relationship with his uncle but knows he is important to his dad, so he always makes an effort to ask about him.

The only person missing from the table is Odell. He never misses Tuesday evening dinner at Grandma's, but he had to work late. Teaching full-time and coaching at the school has always been his dream, but it does mean late nights here and there. With his mom left, his dad seated in front of him, his grandma right, and Ashby and his grandpa at the dinner table too, Adan feels content, soaking in every moment as best he can since he knows this feeling will soon fade into the constant longing and discontentment he knows so well. A reminder of his loneliness deep inside.

Adan finds a moment to slip away from the table after everyone finishes eating to go and start washing the dishes. He can already hear his grandma scolding him before the sink finishes filling up with hot and soapy water.

"Don't you worry about those dishes, boy. That's my job. I asked you to come to eat with us, not do my chores."

"Grandma, we go through this every week. I want to do these dishes; I love to do these dishes," Adan insists. "This is how I say thank you."

"Alright, dear, alright," she says as she retreats to the table.

After draining the sink and placing the dishes back into their cabinet homes, Adan gives his grandparents a hug and a thank you, along with about five "I love yous" before leaving their house. *I wish today were Friday or Saturday so I could stay later.*

Adan's grandparents have a short driveway, but exiting it tonight is an obstacle course considering that he, Ashby, his dad, and his mom all drove separate vehicles. After maneuvering through the cars, he drives the short, five miles home.

Being 20 with a full-time job and still living at home is not cool in Adan's book. Despite everyone saying how smart it is because he can save so much money— which is true—makes it no less embarrassing for him. Despite his embarrassment, he truly is grateful to live at home.

Pulling into the circle driveway and parking in the middle garage, Adan walks into his house, straight to the bathroom to shower and ready himself for bed. Adan is a lark, as he puts it: in bed before 9 p.m. even on weekends. Adan says to people when they ask why he goes to bed so early, "What else is there to do?"

Before calling it a night, Adan walks to the kitchen to say goodnight to Renee. "Night, Mom, love you!" he says, then starts to walk back to his room; Mom is not a hugger.

"Wait," she says. "Tell me about your plans with Kate. Have you decided where you will spend the evening?"

Oh lord, I should have known Mom would want to talk about this.

Adan was set up with Kate by a couple of coworkers. "She is pretty and smart and talented like you," they all said. Adan and Kate started messaging each other back and forth late last week when Adan asked her on a casual date, and she agreed. He tells his mom everything, especially if it involves a girl; her eyes light up with these conversations.

"I booked a reservation at a restaurant overlooking Table Rock Lake in Branson," he answers.

"Oh wow, that sounds nice. Not sure if that could be considered casual, though."

"It is!" he confirms. "I can't take her to just any local restaurant." Mountain View has limited dining options, which have no class level. Branson was the obvious choice for him. "Besides, after dinner, we can take a walk on the Branson Landing." The Landing is an outdoor mall along a lake full of restaurants, shopping, and entertainment. "Kate will love it."

"That's true; she definitely will," she admits. "But she will enjoy it most because of the handsome man she will be spending her evening with."

"Yeah, right; that's why the location has to be so nice; it'll give her something to look at other than this ugly face."

"Adan, shut up. Any girl would be crazy not to fall head over heels for you," she snaps.

"But it's true— "

"And I mean it." She cuts him off. "God has blessed you, don't deny it, and don't think of yourself like that, be confident in who you are, looks included."

"Okay."

"Friday night still, right?" she verifies.

"Yes, taking off work early to drive up there; Kate doesn't work Fridays," he explains.

"I see," she says. "You will have a great time. I don't know how you can always leave work early; I wish I could do that," she whines.

"Well, quit the hospital and take a job as an accountant at a law firm, and you can," he offers.

Although Adan hates his dull job, he likes the flexibility of the schedule.

"From what I hear from you, I'll pass. I must be active and moving all day, sitting like that would turn me into a couch potato."

"What's so bad about couch potatoes?" he jokes.

"Do you really want me to say?" she says with a smirk.

"I guess not; I don't want you to hurt your little couch potato's feelings!"

"Goodnight, Adan. I love you!"

"I love you too, Mom."

TWO

The alarm rings gracelessly at 6 a.m., jolting Adan awake into a dampened mood when he realizes it's only Wednesday. *A whole three days of work left.*

Accounting was his profession of choice; it is, however, annoying to him that a career decision he made at 18 is the one he is stuck with forever. He initially decided to go to college for a degree in business accounting and become a CPA with his own office. When he landed the job at the law firm in town, it solidified that decision even further. In America, if you change your mind about your career, you're a failure, even if the change makes you happier and potentially more successful. But sticking with a job because you chose it first and invested thousands of dollars into it with a college degree is success, even if every day is misery.

Adan is grateful to live in America, though, because at the end of the day, he can make whatever choice he wants, even if it doesn't align with popular culture. As someone who fears negative attention, Adan finds it in his best interest to conform to the culture he lives in and suffer through his job.

It's a good job, he thinks as he peels himself out from under the warm sheets into the cool, crude air in his bedroom. Chills break out all over his body, urging him to lie back down.

A heavy weight is upon Adan most mornings, and today is no exception. Pornography and self-gratification are a devastatingly consequential way to put oneself to sleep. The self-hate that fogs Adan's mind is making it hard for him to even notice the bright morning sun streaming through his window blinds.

As he brushes his teeth, he does so without looking at himself in the mirror, afraid of the monster he will see. But even the dark emotions that swirl in his mind find it difficult to subdue the momentary excitement that fills him when he inhales the sweet aroma of his mom's cinnamon French toast.

Adan finds his way into the kitchen, mood lifted after a hot shower and soon- to-be filled belly. His dad is already at the bar. "Good morning, Mom and Dad," he says with a nod in each direction.

"Morning, Adan," both respond in unison.

"Did you guys sleep well?" he asks as he grabs a plate and fills it with French toast, covering it with butter and syrup.

"Awful," Mom says.

"Don't grow old, Adan," Dad adds. "Too many things to think and stress about when trying to fall asleep."

"Note taken."

Adan's parents don't know about his porn addiction, his tool for falling asleep. He makes sure of that by carefully articulating positive conversations that portray everything in his life as alright. He leaves people with a consistently positive impression; although inside, he is anything but. To justify his behavior, he thinks: *Everyone has secrets.* He is not wrong. Adan's secret is hidden from everyone except himself—well, and of course, God.

After breakfast, Adan does the dishes for his mom. Considering he pays no rent he does meal cleanup with a grateful heart as it is a small price to pay. More than carrying his load at the house, doing the dishes allows his mom to enjoy the art of cooking, not doing the dishes and putting them away. Anything to make life easier for Renee, Adan is more than happy to do it.

"Thank you for cleaning up," Mom says graciously after walking back into the kitchen and putting her hair into a bun.

"No problem."

"I am off to work; see you this evening," she says.

"Okay, love you. Have a good day," he offers.

"Love you too, Adan," she finishes. "Love you, David," she says to his dad on her way out.

Dad is watching the Smithsonian channel as Renee leaves. After returning her "I love you" he turns off the TV and says to Adan, "Let's grab lunch from the new barbecue place downtown. I've heard it's excellent."

"I can make that work. At noon?"

"Yes," his dad confirms. "I'll text Odell and see if he can make it too."

"Sounds like a plan. See you at lunch."

As Adan is packing his bag for work, he includes a new book, and immediately after zipping the bag and tossing it over his shoulder, Ashby groans and blunders out of his room, heading to the bathroom. *The beast is awake.*

Ashby is a couple inches shorter than Adan but double in width. With a love for lifting and protein shakes, he can bench press more weight than every person in his high school at just 15 years old without trying. Granted, the high school has only about 300 students, but even at competitions state-wide, he crushes his opponents without hesitation.

Adan is slim, with "a pot-belly and bubble-butt," as he describes himself. Even though everyone around him considers him fit and good-looking, he only sees himself as full of flaws with much-needed improvement. That is why he spends an hour every day at the gym then harshly criticizes himself any time he skips a day for rest or can't complete the planned reps. It's a never-ending, lose-lose situation.

Wrapping up his so-far ordinary morning, Adan makes his way out of the house to his truck, then makes his mere five-minute commute to work. If traffic is heavy, it might take six minutes, which is the case today.

Once he arrives at work, he strides around the office to give everyone a "good morning." Most of his coworkers appreciate the greeting, thinking it kind and thoughtful. A couple people, however, give him a look of annoyance, which makes it obvious who he will be avoiding today.

I also hate being at work, but at least I don't take it out on someone who is just trying to be nice.

After settling at his desk in his office, he begins making a task list for the day:

Invoices

Outstanding Bills

Update Spreadsheets

The task sheet is so tiny he is grateful for the book he brought. *Going to be another slow day.* As soon as he begins reviewing pending invoices, Naomi waltzes into his office and asks, "Like some coffee, Adan?"

She asks Adan every single day if he would like coffee. His response is always the same. "No, thank you, Naomi."

Naomi and Adan have been with Lester & Associates for nearly 12 months; if she stopped asking now, Adan would worry something was wrong. Clearly, Naomi feels the same. "Are you ready for fall classes to start next week?" Naomi inquires.

Both are taking classes at the local community college; most of Adan's courses are online, with one exception this fall. A seated class is scheduled for Wednesday evenings during the next sixteen weeks, which happens to be shared with Naomi too. "No, not particularly; I've been trying not to think about it," Adan says with a light chuckle.

"Same here." She is pursuing a degree in psychology, and while unsure what she will use it for specifically, she remains at the law firm working as a receptionist. "Are you prepared for our politics elective, the seated class? I hear the professor makes it a cool class."

"No, I haven't even bought the book yet, and I especially hate politics," Adan answers. "But I have also heard the professor makes it interesting, so I am curious about it."

"Me too!" Naomi agrees with a bright smile. "Although you and I will be tired of each other by the end of the day on Wednesdays, considering we will have to work together all day then have to spend the evening together in class."

"That's true. At least our desks aren't right next to each other here at work!"

"Good point, but I will ensure they are at class," she says over her shoulder on her way out of Adan's office to finish serving coffee to the others in the office, or at least he assumes she offers it to everyone the same as him.

The day goes by at its usual pace, and when noon rolls around, Adan finds himself hungry for barbecue. Adan leaves the office and drives to the restaurant, where he finds his dad and Odell standing on the bustling sidewalk waiting for him. *Why are they always early?*

"I work at the school on the other side of town, and you work at an office not a mile from here, yet I still beat you here," Odell fires off at Adan as he makes his way toward them.

"It's been like this for how long now, and you're still surprised?" Adan slams back. He is always late by at least five minutes for everything. He has determined it's because he is an optimist when it comes to time, constantly underestimating the length of time required to travel somewhere or do something.

"Yeah, that is true; not sure why I even notice it anymore."

Odell is six years older than Adan, and apart from the last name, they have nothing in common. Odell is similar in size to Adan, only an inch taller. But he was popular in school and had a multitude of friends. Odell is likable and relatable; people are drawn to him quickly, as people usually are to confident and secure people. Even with their strikingly different personalities, Adan and Odell are close to each other, easily one of each other's best friends.

After making their way inside and finding a table, their waitress arrives quickly, walking with purpose to take their drink orders. Immediately she recognizes the three. "Well, hello there, you guys." She nods to each. "What are you up to today?" It's Lisa, an old friend of Adan's mom and dad. She is easily one of the sweetest people Adan knows.

"We just came in for our usual lunch and wanted to try a new place," Dad says. "How are you, Lisa?"

"Glad you made it in here; it's nice to have your support. And I am doing well; owning a restaurant is hard work but worth it in my book, for now at least," she says with pride and a nervous laugh. "How are you all?"

"Good!" Dad says, and Adan and Odell nod in agreement.

"Good to hear. What can I get you all to drink?"

As she takes their orders, Adan can't help but think how everywhere he goes in this town, even to a brand-new restaurant, he is met with a familiar face, a family friend even. He has never tested the limits of the law or even disobeyed his parents much, for that matter. Even if he wanted to, someone would recognize him and tell his parents before he could even finish whatever it was he was doing. *The joys of living in a small town.*

After ordering their food and receiving their drinks, the trio begins having their typical Wednesday lunch conversation. Dad starts, "I've repaired a quarter of a mile of fence already today; what have you two fellers done?"

Dad is a competitive man, to say the least; he finds it essential to always be busy and productive and likes to talk about it.

"I have almost finished organizing my curriculum for the full school year; it's a lot to go through," Odell challenges.

"Sounds cute," Dad says. Odell rolls his eyes as Dad reveals a big smirk. "Nah, that is a lot of work, I'm sure," he admits.

"I paid ten invoices and made a couple of collection calls to past-due clients," Adan throws in.

"Now that is what I'm talking about!" Dad says sarcastically.

"I would rather be outside helping you," Adan admits. "Being cooped up inside all day sucks."

"Yeah, I would love to be able to work with my boy all day too, but you are setting yourself up for a successful career by working in that office and finishing your degree, and I love that even more."

"Definitely in a good position where you're at, man," Odell chimes in.

"I know; I wish I could be outside more, especially on perfect days like today."

"Definitely understand that. I've always worked outside, and I am not sure I could survive inside all day. When you get old like me, it's hard to accept change," Dad explains. "Change is a part of life, though," Odell mentions.

"I guess it is," Dad admits.

"Here comes the food!" Adan says with a smile; he has grown much hungrier since first heading to the restaurant. Adan ordered a loaded baked potato with sour cream, pulled pork, cheese, and corn salsa. All topped with Devil's Spit BBQ sauce; it is supposed to be the hottest in the area. This is about to become one of his new favorite meals; he can tell just by how his mouth is watering from looking at it. Odell and his dad ordered pulled-pork sandwiches with a mild barbecue sauce. *Wimps.*

Nothing is said while they eat, only grunts signaling they are enjoying their meals or when someone needs a napkin. Once finished, Odell turns his attention to Adan. "So, you're going on a date with Kate Friday?"

"How did you know? Did Mom tell you?"

"No, my friend Charlie told me. He works with her." *Why does Odell always know everyone?*

"Oh, I see. We are going to Branson for dinner, then we'll take a walk through the Landing."

"Wow, that's actually quite romantic."

"Really?" Adan asks. "I thought it was keeping it casual."

"I mean, it's obvious you've put a good amount of thought into how the date will go, and it's a nice place to spend the evening. Casual wouldn't be the word I would use to describe it," Odell explains with excessive hand gestures. "Just know that Kate will likely not consider it casual either."

"Thanks for the tip. I just wanted it to be nicer than a place in Mountain View or any other town within a 100-mile radius." Springfield is the nearest city with nice dining options. It is almost 100 miles from Mountain View, so Adan is used to driving a good hour to two hours to do much of anything cities usually offer.

"I get that," Odell says. "Nothing is wrong with your plan; you're obviously more thoughtful than you realize."

"Thanks, I'll take that as a compliment."

"But, as I said, know that Kate will not think your date is casual, and she will probably expect the second date to be at just as good of a place or better. You're setting some solid expectations for yourself."

"Note taken. I'll worry about a second date after I've seen how the first date goes."

"Awesome," Odell says. "And just so you know, Charlie says Kate is only into guys she thinks have money. Don't let that corrupt your impression of her; that is from someone else."

How am I not supposed to let that influence my impression?

"Wow, some first-class gossip," Dad adds.

"Just wanted you to be aware of how someone who works with her everyday sees her."

"Well, thanks, I guess," Adan says annoyed.

"No problem."

"I need to get back to work, as do you two boys," Dad says, signaling everyone to get up from the table to finish their lunch.

On his short drive back to the office, he can't help but think about what Odell said about Kate. *Does she think I make a lot of money? Is that what my coworkers who set us up told her?*

Adan makes an above-average sum of money, a fair amount he has never told anyone except his parents for fear of jealousy from others. Another reason he feels pressured to stay in the career field he dislikes is the salary. Money is important when it comes to a career.

He has been on many dates but never a second date. Usually, after the first, he finds them to be too immature and annoying. He is mature for his age, or so he is told, so maybe that's why women his age are bothersome to him; he isn't entirely sure. It drives his mom crazy; she wants him to be in a good relationship, and the fact that he isn't causes her to worry. He is a bit lonely, but he knows a forced relationship won't help. He is unhappy; nothing can change that.

When she asks him for the type of girl he is looking for—so she can attempt to set him up— he lists his requirements perfectly clearly:

- Independent
- Athletic
- Driven
- Beautiful
- Creative
- Funny
- Kind
- Loving

Upon reviewing the list, his mom always says he is being too picky, trying to define a "perfect person".

"I am not desperate, so I can be picky," Adan always explains.

He knows you can't judge a person by the gossip you hear about them, even if it is true what Odell said about Kate; he wants to find out for himself by getting to know her at least a little bit.

Once Adan returns to his office, he begins updating some information within company spreadsheets. Although he is the only one who ever updates them and is undoubtedly the only one who looks at them, he finds it important to be diligent. Upon completion, he grabs a bottle of water and begins the new book he brought with him, *Steady Breath*, written by Laramie Clark. It is a self-help book focusing on consistency instead of intensity.

Adan enjoys an engaging book, whether fiction or non-fiction; as long as it has a solid beginning and powerful purpose, he is a fan. He picked *Steady Breath* with no expectations, and within the first few pages, he finds himself challenged to be present in the tasks of the day, both at work and home. Not to be unengaged and wishing to be somewhere else. Laramie uses the quote by C.S Lewis: "The great thing, if one can, is to stop regarding all the unpleasant things as interruptions of one's 'own' or 'real' life. The truth is, of course, that what one calls the interruptions are precisely one's real life."

Realizing that he is guilty of never appreciating moments throughout the day and considering work unpleasant when it is a part of his life is like a punch in the gut. *How can I be so ungrateful?*

Adan silently promises himself he will do better to be present in the moments of the day, considering each moment, even interruptions, as a blessing and a part of his life. Of course, these promises usually last a maximum of a couple of days. *That's why I bought this book, though! This time it will last.*

As 5:00 o'clock presents itself, Adan is finishing the tenth chapter of *Steady Breath*. *I made it all the way to 5 p.m. today!* After completing his rounds to each office to tell everyone "Good evening," he heads home.

On his way home, Adan stops at the grocery store to purchase a few things for his mom. She left work early for once to catch up on some of her chores around the house.

As he nears the driveway of his home, he sees someone in the yard. "Who is that?" Adan thinks out loud. Upon pulling into the driveway and parking, he jumps out of the truck and encounters a scene that knocks all air from his lungs and leaves him speechless.

THREE

A t breakfast, Adan and his dad can't help but laugh when Renee
walks into the room.

"What are you two laughing about now? You did this yesterday,
too."

"We're laughing at the same thing as yesterday," Adan says with a
full smile quickly cut short by another burst of laughter.

Wednesday afternoon, when Adan made it home from work,
he caught his mom mowing the lawn on the riding lawn mower in
her bikini.

"Mom!" he yelled. "What are you doing?"

She looked back at him, clearly embarrassed that her son had
seen her, but accepting there was nothing she could do about it now,
she said, "What does it look like? I am modeling for John Deere."

While Adan is still recalling the hilarious encounter, Renee's face glows red for the countless time in the last two days. "I was expecting to be done before you made it home."

"Why were you embarrassed? Everyone who drove by the house saw you."

"Well, you laughed at me like you are now."

"I'm sorry," Adan struggles to say. "But you have to put yourself in my shoes here. It's impossible not to laugh; you were mowing the lawn in a bikini!"

"Whatever," she says as she turns and walks away, leaving for work.

"I thought you looked sexy, baby," Dad says. "And my opinion is the only one that matters." David turns his head to Adan, and they join in a final round of belly-aching laughter before cleaning up from breakfast and carrying on with their morning routines.

Adan skips his lunch at work so he can leave early using the least amount of PTO possible. By the early afternoon on Friday, the office is slow and quiet. Before he can prop his feet up and start on the final pages of *Steady Breath*, Hannah stops by his office and takes a seat, clearly wanting to talk to Adan about something.

"What's up, Hannah?"

"Hey! Not too much. I wanted to stop by and ask if you and Kate are still going out tonight?" Hannah is the person responsible for setting the two of them up—a nosy but sincere person with the best intentions.

"Yes, we are. Leaving here at 3 p.m."

"Awesome! You two will have a blast; I can't wait to hear all about it on Monday."

"I'll let you know how it goes," Adan says to finish the conversation. Hannah is a good person, he thinks, but she isn't someone he would trust with much personal information. If Adan likes to gossip now and then, Hannah invented it.

With precise timing, almost immediately after Hannah leaves his office, Naomi arrives at the doorway and asks, "Can I talk to you for a second?" Naomi only visits with Adan once or twice a day for small talk, but today, she has come to his office four times; this marks the fifth.

"Sure."

As she takes a seat, Adan can tell something is bothering her. Her usual composure is approachable and warm; right now, however, she seems cold and has a face of steel. Naomi has natural dark and curly hair, a full face, and bright eyes. Adan finds her attractive and is always interested in talking to her, but is surprised when she asks, "Did Hannah set you up with someone?"

Is Naomi jealous?

"Yes, she introduced me to Kate Miller. We are seeing each other tonight. Why do you ask?" Trying to read Naomi's face is impossible; she is revealing nothing except what she wants to.

"Okay, I thought so. Please be careful around Kate; we used to be friends and— anyway, she likes men she can control and who have a lot of money."

Wow, a second time. Not judging Kate prematurely is going to be really hard.

"Surprisingly, it's not the first time I've heard that. Thank you for the heads up. I'm going to go with an open mind, though; it's only fair to allow Kate the room to make her own impression."

"That's fair. I know you are a good person and figured it was only right to tell you." As the words leave her mouth, she regains her usual composure again, making Adan smile at the transformation.

"I appreciate that."

Adan starts to feel guilty a few moments after Naomi leaves his office. *I don't even know Kate yet, and I am already convinced she isn't a nice person.* This is the part of a small town Adan hates. People are quick to project their opinions onto others, not realizing it can negatively influence someone else's perceptions of them. *Nobody asked you, Odell or Naomi.*

At the moment, the clock cries 3 p.m., he is out the door and driving home to change clothes then pick Kate up from her house. She lives 15 minutes south of Mountain View, which will add to the total trip, so he quickly changes his clothes.

On his way to Kate's house, his mom texts him: *Have a good date honey, love you.* He responds, *Love you too.* Shortly after his mom's check-in, his grandma Esme calls him. "Adan, dear, I hope you have a good time tonight."

"Thanks, Grandma. I'll try."

"She will love you; I just know it, but if you don't think she is right for you, that is more than okay; you'll find someone eventually."

Wow. Thanks, Grandma.

"I appreciate that, Grandma; no pressure is good."

"Absolutely, that's all I wanted to say. Bye and love you," she says, ending the call before Adan can return her goodbye.

Adan pulls into Kate's driveway still trying to blot out of his mind what Odell and Naomi said about her. He sends a text to Kate, letting her know he has arrived just as the truck tire touches the driveway. After putting the truck in park, he jumps out to meet her at the door.

Kate still lives with her parents, the same as Adan, and she is five years older than him, which makes him more comfortable with his own living situation. She is still living with her parents because she is saving money. They told her she doesn't have to move out until she is married. Grateful that his living situation won't be an awkward subject, he confidently knocks on the door.

This is a charming house.

When she makes her way to the door, opens it, and comes out onto the deck, he finds himself at a loss for words. She is wearing a pink sundress complimenting her perfectly tanned skin, and she has long and curly dirty-blonde hair. She is wearing big earrings, several bracelets, and a modest necklace. *Oh my God, she is stunning.*

With no greeting other than a smile, Adan takes a step back to allow her room to step off the front patio then meets her at the truck's passenger door, opening it for her.

"Awe, are you opening the door for me?" she asks. Adan can only nod his head. *Get a hold of yourself, man.* "You're so nice," she says as she steps in, and Adan closes the door.

As Adan walks around the truck to get in the driver's seat, he manages seven full, deep breaths, taking his time, hoping it will help him gain a more confident composure. He clambers into the truck with the highest confidence he can manage and says, "You look stunning this evening, Kate, and it is nice to finally meet you in person."

"Thank you so much, Adan, you look nice as well, and I agree it's good to meet you in person too. I'll be honest, I was nervous about tonight, but you seem really great."

How could she be nervous? She could own any room she walked into.

"I am glad you feel that way; hopefully, after a four-hour round trip in the same vehicle, you still feel the same way," he says with a forced chuckle. Branson is at least a two-hour drive one way.

The drive to Branson goes by quickly for Adan, who is fully engrossed in Kate's looks. She has been the one talking for most of the trip, and if you ask Adan what it's been about, you won't find yourself with much of an answer. If he were to see himself from Kate's perspective, he would be surprised if he didn't look like a creep. He can't stop looking at her.

Upon entering the city limits of Branson, Adan reaches for his phone for directions to the restaurant. "What is the name of the restaurant?" Kate asks.

"Lakeview Grille."

"Wow, they were really creative with their name."

"No doubt. It probably took them a while to come up with it!" At this, she laughs, and Adan can't help but blush.

Finding their way to the restaurant doesn't take more than five minutes, and Adan frantically tries to remember anything she said during the drive. All he can recall is that she works as a dental hygienist in West Plains—a town just 30 minutes from Mountain View—and is an only child. Apart from that, he was too absorbed in how pretty she was to remember anything else.

Adan makes Kate wait to get out of the truck so he can exit first, open the door, and help her out. An excuse to hold her hand, even if briefly.

Adan is not the romantic type by any means, and the thought of trying to be stresses him out, but he does take pride in being a gentleman. Not to mention that something about Kate makes him feel he needs to impress her, so he puts on his most charming self possible, which isn't much to brag about. He gracefully walks with her to the restaurant entrance, holding the door for her.

Once they are seated and drinks are ordered, he quickly finds that she is much more intimidating when sitting directly in front of him than at his side.

"Sure is nice in here. Nicer than I expected. Have you been here before?" he asks.

"No, I haven't been here before, but I am surprised, considering how many restaurants I go to."

She probably gets asked out all the time.

"Same," he says. "I actually have a bad habit of eating out; I should cook more of my own meals; it would be much healthier and help my figure, too," he says. *Why did I just turn the conversation subject onto my body?*

"What do you mean? You're ridiculously fit." Adan's eyes light up at the burst of confidence at her compliment.

"Thanks, but I definitely have room to improve."

"I guess that's true for all of us. Hey, look at that lady over there. She has three chins. Oh my gosh, she's huge!"

Adan turns his head to see the lady she is talking about. She is a middle-aged woman eating with her family, and although she is overweight, she is very beautiful.

"Looks like she is the one who needs to eat at home and watch her figure!" Adan says, immediately regretting it. At this, though, Kate laughs so hard she snorts as she tries to keep herself quiet. *I can't believe I just said that. I'm not shallow.* Adan dismisses his momentary guilt from making fun of someone else and returns his full attention to Kate. *She has a nice laugh— not really the contagious kind, though.* She has big brown eyes that lure Adan in, making him feel pressure to keep her attention.

Kate has yet to ask Adan a single question about himself so far into the evening, and he had forgotten entirely about what Odell and Naomi told him until she asks, ""What is your job like?"

"It's a good job, a lot of room for advancement, but currently a little bit boring." *That's the best description I can give.*

"As long as you make good money, it's worth it, right?" *There it is.*

Contemplating how to respond, he decides to test where she is going with this. "Well, considering I only make minimum wage, I wouldn't say it's worth it on the financial side. For me, it's more about the work I do," he lies.

"Oh, but you'll make more as you advance in your career in the company, right?"

"I doubt it; I've heard the max I could ever make there is $35,000 a year." Before Adan can feel guilty about lying again, Kate's body language shifts slightly from warm and friendly, to sharp and cold. Her tone is hollow and disappointed now, whereas before she was overflowing and excited.

"Oh." That is all she says.

Thankfully, the waiter comes with food, and Adan relaxes as he doesn't have to come up with something to say for a few moments.

Kate immediately starts eating, so Adan does the same. The two eat in complete silence, his attraction to her fading by the second. When Adan attempts to start up another conversation, it is quickly killed when she looks up with completely uninterested eyes.

After they finish their meals, Adan asks, "Still up for going down to the Landing?"

"Sure." She is clearly only interested in waiting for the date to run its course and be over.

"We don't have to."

"No, I want to; I'm just a little tired."

They leave the table where, only moments ago, the picturesque sunset captivated Adan's eyes. Now it is an utterly black scene. As they walk past the family, he internally apologizes to her.

Once at the Landing, they shuffle their way through a couple lines of people waiting for a hot air balloon ride and small restaurants. When they make it through the crowds to the main walkway,

Kate finally says, "This place is so beautiful at night," in awe of the lights and water features surrounding them and reflecting on the windows of the storefronts.

"No doubt."

"Thank you for bringing me here; you're really thoughtful."

"Thank you. And thanks for coming with me; it's been a nice evening getting to know you." Adan says it out of good manners more than honest feelings.

"Absolutely," she says with her high-pitched and now empty tone.

Any attraction to Kate that Adan had before is gone; although she is gorgeous, he can't help but be excited for the night to be over. She was so lovely and seemingly interested in him, but in retrospect, she was only interested because she thought he earned a lot of money.

Hannah, we are going to have a heart-to-heart conversation Monday.

After stopping at only a handful of unique shops along the Landing and grabbing a couple of smoothies, they walk back to the truck to make the long drive home. Before they even drive out of the main parking lot, Kate rolls back her seat and shifts into a more comfortable position; once they are on the highway headed toward home, she is already asleep.

Wow, she's definitely into me.

Along the drive home, he remembers how he made fun of a complete stranger to impress Kate. *I feel horrible.* Adan knows first-hand what it is to dislike oneself and one's body. *That lady probably criticizes herself daily for her weight.* Even though internal judgment doesn't affect the other person, it creates a monster out of the one who judges.

After gladly dropping Kate off at her house, he finishes the drive home.

When he comes into the house, he finds his mom.

"Mom? You're still awake this late at night?" She is wearing her "Queen's Robe," as she calls it, and she is sitting confidently on her favorite side of the couch watching HGTV.

"Yes. You thought I'd go to bed having not heard about how your date went? You must not know me very well," she says with a sly smile.

Adan knew without a doubt she would be waiting for him. She does it anytime he is out later than his usual 7 p.m. He loves coming home and talking to her; Mom always makes everything seem better with her outrageous amount of optimism.

"I knew you would be, just thought you would have given up on me by now since it's past midnight."

"Nope. Now sit down and talk to me."

He finds his favorite chair, which sits at a near-perfect 90-degree angle from where his mom is seated. "It was horrible," he starts as he leans back into the chair.

"Why was it horrible?" she asks.

"Mom, she slept the whole way home." Her eyes open wide as she throws her head back with mouth agape. Laughter erupts out of her like a volcano. Adan can't help but laugh at the reality of it now too. "It is pathetic but funny," he says.

"Were you that boring?"

"No. Maybe. By mid-date, she lost all interest in me."

"Why is that?"

"Because Odell warned me, she was only into guys with money. And when the topic of work came up, I lied and commented on how I only make minimum wage."

"Adan!" she gasps.

"Anyway, before that part of the conversation she was all friendly and engaged, but afterward, she slowly grew into a cold brick."

"I'm so sorry, honey," she offers.

"It's okay; I was hoping it wasn't true. But I should have known; small-town gossip and rumors are usually true."

"Oh no, they are not. That is so kind of you to have given her a chance to make her own impression on you. Just because this time it happened to be true doesn't mean that's always the case. Many people would have believed the rumors first, but you didn't. That is because you have character."

Guilt ensues about what he said about the beautiful lady at the restaurant. "You wouldn't say that if you knew what I said when I was still trying to impress her and make her laugh."

"What do you mean?"

"First, Kate is gorgeous, and when I saw her, I was worried I wouldn't be able to speak, but finally, my head started working properly again, and I mustered up some confidence. But second, she was not a genuinely nice person because she made a mean comment about a beautiful woman's chins."

"Plural?"

"Yes. When Kate made fun of the woman's chins, I added a snarky comment and made her laugh. I participated in making fun of a complete stranger behind their back; I'm an awful person."

"That isn't who you are; you were just caught up in the moment, trying to make a good impression on someone you thought you might like. Everyone is guilty of that."

"But something about it is really bothering me."

"Well, it was wrong of you, but like I said, you aren't like that; you are sweet and kind and see the good in people. Forgive yourself and move on."

Forgive me? Not a chance.

Adan sees the good in people and is quick to forgive others for their mistakes, even if they wrong him in the process. But self-forgiveness does not exist in Adan's mind, and he can only see the bad in himself. The way he judged the lady earlier in the night, he will be sure to judge himself at least twice as brutally from now on.

"You are too nice to me, Mom. I will try."

"So, who is Naomi?" she asks with a glittering smile.

"Nope, not tonight," he says, standing up from the chair.

"*I'm* just kidding around. But seriously, you do need to find a good girl eventually."

Eventually. There it is again.

"Mom, I am only 20, I have plenty of time, and I'm not desperate."

"You're right. You're still young, but you're way too picky. I'm worried you're going to start feeling alone."

"How could I be lonely? I have you, Dad, Odell, and Grandma and Grandpa," he says as he sits back down.

"Yes, but you can be surrounded by family and friends whom you love and love you and still feel alone. You need someone to be intimate with, not just sexually, but more than that, relationally. You need someone you can talk to that you trust with all your secrets."

"That's overrated; I'm fine."

"I know there are secrets that you have, Adan," she says as if she can see right through him. "Things that bother you that you don't talk to anyone about. These secrets will separate you and overtake you, and I don't want that to happen. I want my baby boy to have someone he can be intimate with."

I do too, but nobody deserves that. Not even my worst enemy would deserve to be stuck with someone like me. Being alone only hurts me, which is how it should be.

Adan has always admired his mom's wisdom, which never fails to reveal itself at the perfect time. "Maybe I will someday, Mom. But for now, please stop worrying about me. If the right woman is out there, I will find her; it'll happen in its own time."

"I will pray that is the case, Adan. I will pray," she says with her seriousness gone and her smile back.

Prayer is undoubtedly useless. People saying rehearsed lines before eating, or before and after church service, doesn't seem to achieve anything. From Adan's perspective, prayer is more of a show than a form of authenticity. If it is authentic, it is just someone treating God like a genie, asking Him to do something for them or someone else. Adan believes in God, of course, and calls himself a Christian, but that is as far as it goes for him. Knowing his mom, though, her prayer will be authentic, still useless, but authentic, nevertheless.

FOUR

Saturday mornings always prove to be a favorite of Adan's. He is able to—like most of the workforce in America who work 9 to 5 jobs—sleep in. For him, 7 a.m. sharp is as late as his body will let him sleep. Without an alarm, he rises and opens his blinds to let the sunlight in.

The typical shame cycle is in effect this morning, just like any other day, but he is becoming more familiar with the feeling. He isn't seeing a way to stop his submission to the temptation of pornography anytime soon, so perhaps it's just as well that he gets used to waking up and feeling like a pile of shit.

To his surprise, he has a text from Odell. It's a surprise because the whole family will be at Grandma's for breakfast, as they are every Saturday. They'd usually talk there.

"What are you doing today?" Odell's text asks. **"Nothing,"** Adan responds.

"Want to go to Eminence to float? After breakfast at Grandma's, obviously," Odell asks. "Sure, see you in a few," Adan accepts.

"Okay, I'll call and reserve two kayaks. See you in a few," Odell finishes.

Adan and Odell go floating multiple times each summer. The Jack's Fork River—the closest option—loses most of its depth and current by August. The Current River is fed by so many springs that it stays plenty deep and maintains a strong flow of water, making it the perfect river to float on today. Even though it is a longer drive, it is worth it.

Floating on the rivers of the Ozarks is easily the best form of entertainment one can find in the area. It's cheap, fun, easily accessible, and you can always count on a good tan or horrible sunburn.

At Grandma's house, three brothers participate in an all-out eating contest to see who can eat the most biscuits. Adan can usually chow down on four, but Odell and Ashby can effortlessly eat six or more. Today, though, Adan only eats three, and Odell does the same. Neither wants to look like a bloated seal out on the river.

After breakfast, Adan runs back home to change into swim trunks and a cut-off shirt and packs a bag full of light snacks and water, along with two towels and sunscreen. He finishes this in a rush and heads to town to meet his brother at his house. After honking a solid five times— four for good measure—he puts the truck in park so Odell can climb in, and they can leave.

With the extra 35-minute drive to the Current River past Eminence, Adan and Odell fill the space with a conversation about his date with Kate, which Odell prides himself upon having had an accurate forecast about. They had grown up together for Adan's entire life and Odell's from when he was six. Odell is easily his best friend; talking comes naturally between them, and neither holds anything back when it comes to giving the other a hard time. Even an embarrassing date is not off-limits.

"What'd I tell you?" Odell smarts off.

"You were right, I admit it," Adan forfeits.

"Don't let that awful thing you're still calling a date make you feel bad. She is not someone you'd want to be with anyway."

"True, but she was so hot!"

"I know! I might have stalked her on social media after Charlie told me you were going on a date just to make sure she would be good enough for you. I'm sure your eyes were gushing hearts whenever you looked at her."

"Yes, I couldn't stop looking at her; she captivated me." Adan swoons.

They arrive at Doug's Canoe Rental with only three minutes to spare. As Odell runs inside to pay for their rental kayaks, Adan gathers their things into a packable load. Stirring dust into the air, the van arrives to take them to the launch point a few miles down the road, just as Odell is hurrying out of the building.

The drive to the launch point is only about ten minutes, but Adan is beyond ready to get out of the van. He feels carsick. Grateful to finally arrive, they unload their kayaks, climb in, and push off into the water, paddling to align themselves with the river's current. The best part of floating the Current River is that it is broad and swift enough to carry a kayak along without effort except to steer around a rock or tree every so often.

The total float trip usually takes six hours with stops, but they do it in only five since they skip lunch and snack along the way. Adan spends most of the float sprawled backward, giving it his best to lie flat along the kayak. With his hat over his face, he is carried along the river steadily without a single worry. As they are nearing the middle of the trip, they float by multiple, impossibly blue-hued springs, enormous Ozark Mountain bluffs covered in glowing moss, and a plethora of dark caves. These never fail to create awe and wonder in Adan's mind.

Odell typically shuffles himself down just enough to support his neck and head so he can snooze down the river. Today though, he is perked up, like he has something pressing on his mind requiring his attention.

"Adan," he says.

"Yes…"

"I have some pretty cool news."

"Really? What is it?" Adan asks as he sits up and readjusts his hat to look at his brother.

"I got my dream job this week."

"I thought your dream job was to be a teacher?" he says, perplexed.

"Yes, but I got a job at the high school in Bolivar as the head football coach." Odell manages without making eye contact.

"Bolivar, Missouri?"

"Yes."

"That's three hours away, Odell; how will you make that work?" Adan's stomach falls out from beneath him.

"I'm moving there."

"You're kidding," Adan says.

"Adan, this was the hardest thing I have ever had to tell anyone, but it's what I have always wanted, and I've accepted the job."

"Is this why you wanted to go floating today, so you could sucker punch me?"

"Adan, they called me Tuesday, and I didn't know how to tell you. It all happened so fast."

"But you can't go. You're my best friend," Adan says as tears start burning his eyes.

Odell is already crying. "I'm so sorry, Adan. This is the right thing for me, you know that. Better benefits and pay and I would be the *head* football coach; you know that's been my dream my whole life." Adan knows it would be good for him and that it is his dream, but he refuses to accept it.

"What am I supposed to do?" he asks with a wavering voice.

"I'll come visit every other weekend. Adan, I love you, man. You are an incredible person; let yourself make new friends. You don't have to replace me, but just allow other people into your life who you want to be around."

"I don't make friends as easily as you do, Odell. It's impossible to make friends when you're as big of a loser as me," Adan manages to say with a fading voice.

"Adan, you're not a loser. You are, without a doubt, the coolest guy I know, and I'm not just saying that because you're my brother."

"Yeah, right. Someone whose best friend leaves them for a stupid, fucking job is a loser in my book."

"Adan, I…"

"I don't want you to sympathize with me; I don't want to talk anymore either." He paddles at least 50 feet ahead and lets the reality of losing his brother and dearest friend settle in. For the rest of the float trip, not a word is spoken between the two.

Once loaded back into the truck to head home, Odell asks, "Want to go to the Dairy Shack?"

The Dairy Shack is the hotspot of Eminence, a fast-food restaurant that supernaturally "hit the spot".

"No," Adan says.

After a few minutes into the drive back to Mountain View, Adan has determined he is being selfish and childish. He knows how good of an opportunity this will be for Odell. *But how will I make it without seeing and talking to him daily?*

"When do you start?" Adan asks.

"This Wednesday."

"How will you find a place to live that soon?"

"I'm going to stay with my friend Zach until I find a place; he has a spare bedroom in his apartment."

"I see."

"I really didn't want to upset you, Adan. You have no idea how hard this is on me too. But there is no denying this is what I should do. What I was meant to do." Odell is being honest; growing up, all Adan heard out of his mouth was something related to football. He knows it is his dream, but it isn't making this any easier for him to accept.

"I'm happy for you; you'll do great."

"Thanks, that means a lot. And, I promise, I will come home every other weekend, and we will stay in touch over the phone the same as we do now."

"Okay."

"And what you said earlier about being a loser and it being hard to make friends, man, nothing could be further from the truth."

"Odell, look at me; look at my lifestyle. I am a weird person. I am like a middle-aged man already with an established career in the process; I go to bed by 8:00 o'clock every night." *I might as well be bald; it would suit me.* "Oh, and I have no friends. You couldn't understand, because friends come easily to you, but they don't to me. I have my family, and that's only because they *have* to like me."

"You are not weird. You're more mature than anyone I know; you are kind, respectful, responsible, and the most thoughtful person. Yeah, you're almost nothing like other guys your age, which makes it more difficult to find friends, but that doesn't make you weird. If you give other people a chance instead of keeping everyone at a distance, you can build a solid friendship with anyone you want."

"And when it comes to finding a girlfriend and eventual wife, don't stress. You might have a hundred more dates with girls like Kate before you find the person. Look at me; I'm 26 and single. We're both picky, but that's a good thing."

"Thanks Odell, that's nice of you to say."

"Don't compare yourself to other people. Who cares if you're different. God made every one of us unique, so it's good that you don't 'fit in.'"

Adan has never "fit in". Not at any point during high school or up until now. Always interested in numbers more than others are and uninterested in sports. He liked, and still does, being active and working out, but that was considered useless unless you played a sport. He has spent twenty years as a unique person, always noticed and generally well-liked, but has never been a part of a group or any meaningful relationships outside his family. At least he has a good family; come to the end of the day, family matters most.

"Thank you, Odell. And I'm sorry I was too angry to have a good time on the last half of the float trip."

"It's okay. I was ready to just be done too."

When back at his home after dropping Odell off in town at his house, Adan finds Mom cooking cheeseburgers for dinner.

"Hey, Mom."

She turns her face toward him with softness in her eyes. "Hey, honey, did you and Odell talk?"

"Yes. You already knew he was moving?"

"He told your dad and me last night." After saying this, she begins to cry, which she does not often do, and her tears cause Adan's eyes to well up with tears too.

"I'm gonna miss him, Mom," Adan says through harsh sniffling.

"I know. Me too," she says as she walks toward him and wraps her comforting arms around him, and they each cry together at the thought of a son and a brother moving away.

Tonight, Adan isn't tempted to use pornography. He cries himself to sleep.

FIVE

The following days after Odell's departure were excruciatingly
difficult for Adan. There wasn't a day in his life when Adan can
remember Odell not being close by. Even when Odell was in college,
the university was only a short drive from Mountain View.

He spent the entire weekend helping Odell pack his essential
clothes and other small furniture into his truck, and on Monday,
he followed him to Bolivar to Zach's house and helped him unload
everything into his new home for the time being.

Once they finished unpacking from the truck, the reality of the
situation hit Adan again, and he had to find a moment of privacy to
collect himself. He was powerless against what he was experiencing
in that moment.

"Hey, are you alright?" Odell asked Adan who was trying to hide
at the back of the truck.

"Oh yeah, I'm fine."

Odell grasped Adan's shoulder pulling him in for a hug. "I love you, Adan. It's gonna be hard on me not seeing you every day." *You have no idea.* "Make sure you always answer the phone when I call, and I'll do the same."

"Love you too. I will."

By the time Wednesday rolls around, Adan is grateful that classes have started. They keep his mind occupied after work, so he has less time to think about his brother. He wouldn't have time to see Odell anyway with both work and school and that makes him feel slightly better. They've talked over the phone for the last two days. Odell started his job the same day as Adan's seated class, which begins at 5:15 p.m. Instead of a phone call for the sake of today's busy schedule, he sends a text: **"Good luck today, Odell, your new students and athletes will love you!"**

Odell replies, **"Thank you, Adan; I sure hope so! Have a good day today also; love you, man."**

Naomi stops by his office multiple times today, as usual. He would never admit it to her for the sake of embarrassment, but he really does enjoy talking to her throughout the day. Her personality is so upbeat and optimistic, and her smile could light up the darkest room. "Today is the day! Are you ready to learn about politics for the next sixteen weeks?" she asks.

"You know I am. What about you?" Adan responds.

"Well, considering I am going to be running a campaign to be a state representative next year, I am. Might learn something important," she says with a straight face.

"Are you serious? That's awesome, but I never thought of you being in politics!"

Her face lights up like she won a prize. "Don't tell me you believed me?" she says with a growing grin.

"No..." Adan says, embarrassed by his gullibility. "Well, maybe you *should* become a politician; you're a good liar." He turns his face back to his computer.

"Thanks; I'll keep that in mind if every other job on earth is taken."

With this, they laugh, and Naomi walks away. *Off to visit with the other coworkers,* he assumes.

By the time 5:00 o'clock makes its presence known, Adan is already on his way to the college in downtown Mountain View, a three-minute drive from the office. Naomi pulls into the parking spot next to Adan's; she drives a bright orange Toyota RAV4 which matches her personality perfectly.

They walk into the college building together, inhaling the aroma of a freshly cut lawn, and guessing who they will potentially share the class with, silently grateful for each other's company. Her familiar face promises to bring a level of comfort in a new place. Naomi laughs at most of the things Adan says when he isn't even trying to be funny, but her laughter urges him to keep trying his best jokes, knowing he will be rewarded with her contagious laugh.

Once they are in the classroom, they find a seat at the same table and observe the room's layout and their classmates already seated. Predetermining who they will pair up with if groups are required by their professor.

At exactly 5:15, the professor walks in. He is a short, older man, mostly bald, with a round and kind face. *He looks wise.* Without first greeting the class, he begins setting up his teaching podium with multiple pens, notepads, and books.

Finally establishing his place satisfactorily in the front of the room, he looks up, smiles and says, "Good evening, class. It is good to see and be here with you all," Adan can't help but admire the soft tone of his voice, clear and intriguing. "My name is Paul Sage; I would like to request that you call me Paul. None of that Professor Sage nonsense," he says as he walks around the podium. "I'm going to take a moment to briefly introduce you all to my life; after I'm done, we will go around the room so that each of you can do the same." Adan's palms start sweating. He hates public speaking, especially if it's talking about himself.

"I was born and raised in Boring, Oregon. Yes, there is a town called Boring, but it isn't *boring*. It is one of the most beautiful places in America. It's a small, close-knit community, which is why my wife, and I were drawn to Mountain View; we love being close and involved in the community and with the people we live around.

"From a young age, I always wanted to teach, but that wasn't the road I was meant to take out of high school. I went to Law School, became an attorney, and worked at a law firm for ten years in Seattle, Washington. Which is where I met my beautiful wife, Lily. After that, I became the owner of that same law firm. Fast-forward to now, 20 years later. I have decided to semi-retire, teaching American Government and Politics as a part-time job here at the university. Been doing so for three years now. Finally living my original dream.

"The laid-back vibe of the Ozarks is just what we've always wanted for ourselves at the time of retirement. Now..." he trails off as he finds the roster to call on the first student to introduce themselves. "Emilia Johnson." A small-framed girl with blond hair stands up. She was a couple years younger than Adan in high school, but he recognizes her. This is her first college class, and she is pursuing her general education because she hasn't yet confirmed the career she is most interested in. *That sounds like Naomi.* He smirks at her.

"Dante Reed."

After ten more students introduce themselves to the class, not in alphabetical order, Paul finally calls out, "Adan Caddell." Adan has already rehearsed what he will say; it's the same speech he uses for his online class introductions.

"Hi, my name is Adan Caddell. I live here in Mountain View, and I have my whole life. I work as an accountant at Lester and Associates law firm," he says, giving an acknowledging glance to Paul, who smiles. "I am pursuing a bachelor's degree in business; and hopefully, I'll be able to become a CPA with my own office."

Before he can sit down, Paul asks, with a hint of disappointment saturating his tone, "Is that all?"

"Yes," Adan says, shocked to even be asked.

"You seemed like you had more to say." He turns his attention to the woman next to him. "Naomi Moore."

Adan is embarrassed by Paul, feeling singled out. But his embarrassment quickly fades when Naomi stands up, and all eyes move to her. *She looks so confident.*

"My name is Naomi Moore; it's nice to be in class with all of you. A little about myself. I was born in Austin, Texas. As a child, my parents, siblings, and I moved to many different states and cities but finally settled here in Mountain View a couple of years ago. I've taken most of my college classes online due to us moving around so much, but I am glad to have a seated class, with this being my final semester. I'll graduate at the end of this Fall with a bachelor's degree in psychology."

"I'm not yet sure where I want to work, but until I do, I am working at Lester and Associates as a receptionist with Adan." As she finishes the last sentence, she looks at Adan and smiles proudly.

After a few more introductions, Paul resumes his teacher role. "Since our time is mostly spent for this evening, we will have a class discussion then call it a night. I will ask everyone a couple of questions as a class, and I want each of you to participate in the discussion and break down the question. My preferred method of teaching is through conversation."

I'm gonna like this class, Adan thinks.

Paul finds his way back behind the podium, puts his glasses on to read, then takes them off and asks, "Who in here believes, by a show of hands, that burning the American Flag should be legal?"

What in the world? What kind of question is that?

Nobody raises their hand.

Adan knows there is a purpose for this question, more than just the answer.

"Ok, let me ask this," Paul carries on. "How many of you believe it should be legal to choose if you go to church and what church you go to?" Everyone raises their hands; mumbling fills the room.

It's as if a lightbulb turns on in Adan's head, and he realizes the meaning behind the question. After the class drops their hands, Adan raises his.

"Adan," Paul acknowledges. "Do you want to ask a question, or do you think I shouldn't be able to choose what church I go to?"

"It should be legal to burn the American flag. Although I consider it disrespectful, it is a form of free speech. The same as I believe it should be legal for people to choose if and which church they attend. The freedom to do either is what America is all about."

"That is insightful of you, Adan. Thank you for sharing," Paul says. "Adan somewhat caught on to my point, but yes, it is legal to burn the American flag as it is a form of freedom of speech. It is also legal to choose where you go to church if you go."

A swell of pride pulses through Adan at the fact of being right.

"The freedom to choose is not dependent on whether it's a popular or unpopular opinion; America is known for our ability to make our own choices. But as you will learn throughout this class, our freedoms are slowly being deteriorated by lawmakers whose personal opinions interfere with how they write the law." Paul is on a roll and begins to pace the room. "You will learn the rights we have, the ones we don't, and the ones we should or shouldn't have. Be prepared to be active in the discussion; this is where the passing or failing grade comes from."

"Let's call it a night, shall we? This old man is tired." The entire class whispers under their breath in agreement.

As Adan gets up to leave, he says goodnight to Naomi, but before he can walk out of the classroom, Paul shouts at him. "Adan, come here for a second if you don't mind."

"Sure," Adan says hesitantly.

Naomi glances at him as she leaves and points as if he is in trouble for bad behavior.

When it is just Adan left in the room, Paul starts. "Adan, you strike me as someone special."

Adan smiles.

"I appreciate your participation in tonight's discussion. You are the first student I've had here that hit my point squarely on the head."

"You're the first teacher I've ever had that teaches in such a way that a person has to actually think and figure out something for themselves."

"I'm glad you like my form of teaching," Paul says.

"I'm really excited for what the rest of this class brings. I always assumed the purpose of government was to *enforce* my beliefs when actually its purpose is to *protect* my beliefs."

Paul steps backward. "Wow. You can teach this class if you'd like," Paul says with excitement. "Really, though, I'm going to enjoy having you in my class; your insights seem to surpass your age. What are you, 22?"

"I'm 20."

"Wow, just wow. What you said a moment ago took me a solid forty years to understand; you're going to excel in life."

Something about the way Paul is talking to Adan is building up his confidence and making him more secure in his own skin as he stands here. *This is a remarkable old man.*

"Thank you, Paul. That is kind of you to say."

"Say, what are you doing tonight for dinner?" Paul asks.

"Probably just eat whatever I can find in the fridge; my mom doesn't cook on Wednesday nights."

"Perfect. Would you like to come to eat dinner with my wife and me?"

Usually, Adan is a homebody, especially when going somewhere with people he doesn't know. He will find any excuse to not go and stay home. But he feels comfortable around Paul and is really enjoying talking to him. Surprising himself, he says, "Sure, that sounds nice. Thank you."

"My pleasure. If you want to follow me, I live only a few miles out of town."

The first thing Adan notices when pulling into Paul's driveway is the enormous flower beds, unimaginably detailed, surrounding not only the small home but the trees and entrance gates. The landscaping and flowers work masterfully together in representing the heart of their creators.

Something about the plants and flowers and their purposeful design reminds Adan of when he was a child. He would exclaim with great joy as if he had found a pot of gold at the end of a rainbow. Constantly worrying his mom at first with his shout, who would quickly come to him and make sure he was okay only to find that he was admiring a little flower of some kind. He would always tell his mom, "It's the prettiest flower in the world, Mommy!" He has since outgrown the excitement of such a small thing, but it brings a smile to his face, nonetheless. On the other hand, his mom wishes daily that her little Adan could find joy and wonder in such small things again.

He parks the truck and follows Paul into his house. The moment he steps inside, his senses are delighted, not only by the smell of yeast bread baking but also by the incredible atmosphere of the room that must have been done only by the most creative person alive. Splattered throughout are little knick-knacks, colorful pillows on the furniture, books, Rustin linens, and other small items crafting a grand theme of nature and possibility. On the walls are ambient watercolor paintings with no recognizable structure but captivate Adan's eyes. Everything is somehow balanced with the gardens outside the home, carefully intertwined, creating an even more dramatic effect on those who have the privilege to see such a masterpiece of a room.

"This is beautiful," Adan says in awe.

"Thank you," Paul says proudly. "Lily works hard to keep the house decorated but still comfortable."

Adan follows Paul into the kitchen and dining room. *How can a person possibly create a space like this? Mom would love this. Who wouldn't?* Just being in the room is captivating, but when Lily walks into view, Adan is left speechless.

Lily is a woman of great height with broad shoulders. Her dreadlocks are to her lower back, and her smile is bold and sincere. She is wearing a homemade gown—if that's what you call it— with sewn-in flowers, leaves, natural rocks, and dirt splashed in between. "You must be Adan," she says with a deep and powerful voice.

"Guilty." He reaches out his hand to shake hers, but before his hand makes it very far into the space between them, she steps forward and pulls him into a bear hug as if he were a lost child.

"It's nice to meet you, Adan; sorry, I'm a hugger," she says as she peels herself back. "I don't like that ole handshaking; that's for strangers."

Unless I am mistaken, we've never met. Adan, partly taken aback by such an intense hug, only grins in response.

"I love your smile, boy; never stop smiling like that," she says as she steps back into the kitchen to finish preparing the food.

"Have a seat and make yourself at home, Adan. Food will be ready soon," Paul says. "About five minutes," Lily shouts from behind the stove in the kitchen. *I never knew people could be so welcoming to non-family members.*

Paul steps out of the room for a moment, and Adan is easily entertained by just gazing at the artwork and creations around him. "Lily, I am blown away by your home; this is unlike anything I've ever seen."

"I appreciate that, Adan. I enjoy painting and mixing different-colored objects in the most off- the-wall ways. Keeps life interesting."

"I'm sure it would..." he says as his eyes land on photographs of who he assumes is Paul and Lily's family, thoughtfully placed inside the squares of a stained-glass window. "Are these your children?" he asks Paul when he comes back into the room.

"Sure are." Pointing to each person in the picture, he explains, "the oldest boy's name is Drazic, the middle boy is Joe, and the little doll here is Ava."

"You have a beautiful family. Are you two grandparents yet?" he asks.

"The proudest!" Lily sings from the kitchen.

Paul walks to his desk beside the dining room table and pulls out a large binder full of pictures.

"Adan, you had no idea what you were getting yourself into when you agreed to let us host you for dinner, but you're about to find out!" he exclaims as he begins narrating the pages of pictures.

"He won't want to come back, Paul," Lily says with a grin.

"Actually, I would love to see and hear about your family." Adan is comfortable at Paul's home and is especially interested in their lives. Something about these two is beyond description. All he knows is he is content in this place at this moment with these people. He isn't content often, so he soaks up every second he can.

As Paul finishes boasting about his family and pictures, he, Adan, and Lily eat a wonderfully prepared meal of corn on the cob, homemade rolls, and tender roast beef. "This is some of the best food I've ever eaten, Lily; you are an amazing cook!" Adan exclaims after just his first bite.

"Thank you, Adan; I appreciate that."

Once they are done eating and Adan answers a few questions about his family, he decides to ask a question that he is sure he already knows the answer to. *They are the kindest people I've ever met; they have to go…* "So, where do you two go to church? Anywhere in Mountain View?"

"Actually, we don't attend a church," Paul says plainly. *Oh, this is awkward.* "But we both deeply love the Lord."

Lily adds, "Oh yes, Jesus is my everything."

Adan looks at them without trying to look confused but failing miserably. "So, you're Christians?"

"That is for you to decide," Paul responds confidently.

Adan, no longer trying to hide his confusion, asks, "How so?"

"It is in the latter half of Acts 11:26, 'And in Antioch, the disciples were first called Christians.' You see, the disciples followed Jesus; they loved him. They were called Christians by other people, who many theologians theorize originally meant as an insult; the disciples took no offense to the name but instead embodied it. Christian means 'little Christ.'"

"Lily and I don't call ourselves Christians but allow others to call us such, proudly wearing the name when they do."

Awe-struck by such an interesting way of living, Adan tries his best to understand it. Paul, who can tell he isn't quite sure, continues. "To us, the relationship is everything, and please don't take this as though I'm over-generalizing the churches in Mountain View or anywhere for that matter. But the church is currently more focused on the production, whether small or large, on Sunday mornings than the relationship with our Father that we were created for."

"I have always called myself and considered myself a Christian from childhood. This is a lot to take in," Adan admits.

"Adan, please do not think that the way we choose to live is by any means the right way. A person's culture and family upbringing, or lack thereof, greatly influence their relationship with God."

"The way you keep talking about your relationship with God makes me question whether I even have one," he says with a light chuckle.

"Well then, how would you describe your relationship with God?"

"I don't know."

"You don't have to answer immediately, but you can think about it. For me, Father is my greatest friend, my favorite person to spend time with," Paul says, smirking at Lily. "He is my source of joy; everything I do involves Him." *Wow.*

"For me," Lily starts in, "Jesus is my heart, my mind; he influences my every action and every breath. I talk to him endlessly throughout the day. His spirit is my inspiration and my creativity." *Are these people even human?*

Adan contemplates his relationship with God. Technically, he thinks, everyone has a relationship with God, intimate or distant. Adan doesn't know God personally, but his impression of God is limited to what the preacher taught at the church he grew up in. Like most people, he believes attending church constitutes what being a Christian is. But now that he thinks about it, he is just a good church attendee, more than a follower of Christ.

The church is always the same, calculable, planned, and controlled, even down to the tithe-giving sales pitch at either the beginning or end of service. Slowly he realizes Paul and Lily are onto something. Churches, or at least all the ones he has attended himself, really are focused on the Sunday morning service.

"You're right. Churches are seemingly obsessed with the production they provide."

"It has come to that at most, it seems. However, they do have good intentions, at least," Lily responds.

"I guess they do," Paul says with an unsure shrug. "So, Adan, how would you describe your relationship with God?"

He is tempted to just say "good" and continue criticizing the church but feels compelled to tell the truth. "Not great," he says, surprised by his honesty.

"Why is that?" Paul presses.

Now Adan thinks about this question as he looks down at the table with forceful focus. This question threatens to expose him to the fraud he believes himself to be. It would reveal the part of himself he works so hard daily to conceal from everyone around him. His face is burning, his palms sweating, and his heartbeat pumping out of his chest. He doesn't have the cunning to stop himself before he admits, "I'm not a very good son." Crying now with ugly tears and a squeezed face, he can feel his sinuses clogging up. *What am I doing?* He wishes he could stop this embarrassment, unsure how he could have fallen apart so easily in front of two people he barely knows.

Paul looks at Adan, who is now sobbing in his chair at the dinner table and places a hand on his shoulder. "Adan. Let it out." *Let it out? This isn't intentional!* "What you just said was a lie you've been believing. Nothing could be further from the truth."

Adan can barely speak through his tears and sniffling; he lifts his eyes to meet Paul's, whose eyes are filled with grace and kindness as he looks at Adan, undoubtedly embarrassed and emotionally exposed. "It isn't a lie, though. I am a disappointment; I'm not worthy of a relationship like you have with God," he barely gets out.

"Adan, do you believe God's word in Genesis, when God looks upon his creation each day after he creates and 'saw that it was *good*'?"

"Yes."

"You are a part of that creation. You, Adan, are a good creation of God. Anything that says otherwise is a lie, a misconception of who you are; that is what sin is."

Adan is beginning to recompose himself again, unwilling to open up to them about anything more profound—specifically his pornography addiction—although tempted. *I feel safe here.*

"Believe that, Adan, because it's true. You are a good creation."

Adan nods his head in agreement.

"Come here, son," Lily says as she walks over to him from her side of the table and hugs him tightly. "I can see the good flowing out from you, dear; it'll take time to change how you see yourself, but right now is the start. Remind yourself every day that you are what?"

"A good creation." Adan smiles honestly, feeling like a child, but in a good way.

His smile warms his whole body and seeing the careful attention he receives from Paul and Lily, his heartbeat slows, and his breathing deepens. *I am safe here.*

After a few minutes of continued positive reinforcement from Paul and Lily, Paul excuses himself from the table to retrieve something from his bedroom and office.

He carries a tan leather book-sized notebook in its plastic wrapping when he returns. When Paul places it squarely on the table in front of him, he notices the words engraved on it: Daily Kairos.

"What is this?" Adan asks.

"That there is a journal created to deepen the participant's relationship with God. You'll notice simple and elegant prompts to help guide you."

"This a very nice gift. Thank you."

"You're more than welcome. Feel no pressure to use it, but I can tell you are longing for more in life, and I know you'll find what you're looking for within a relationship with your Father, Jesus, and Holy Spirit."

Adan, still unsure how he could ever think of himself as good, finds the idea of knowing God better desirable. After thanking the Sages many times over for both dinner and an unexpected emotional breakdown, he leaves the indescribable beauty of their home to make the drive to his.

At home, he is unsurprised to find his mom waiting for him. This time she is reading a book and has her glasses on which reflect the pages she is focused on. With her long dark brown hair flowing over her shoulder, Adan can't help but acknowledge her royal appearance.

My mom is so beautiful.

A quarter after ten is late for Adan, but she doesn't press him for answers on his whereabouts, so he doesn't delve into the details, still needing to sleep on the events and let them settle first.

After they offer each other goodnight farewells, he ends the long day back in his room, carefully placing his new journal on his dresser top. Before going to bed, he intentionally sets his alarm 30 minutes earlier than usual.

He has a mix of anticipation and fear about the new journal and the expectations he has for it.

He might have finally found everything he has ever wanted.

No pressure, God.

SIX

At the sound of the alarm, Adan is startled awake like usual. After turning it off and rolling out of bed, the typical shame attempts to overwhelm him, and he is prepared to let it, but remembers the journal Paul gave him last night. As the memory lands in his mind, excitement fills him. He quickly goes through part of his morning routine, a splash of water waking him up so he can be as present and focused as possible.

The aroma of freshly steeped green tea fills the room—usually drunk at breakfast but much needed now to gain focus. He peels the journal from its plastic wrapping with a strong expectation. His hands run the length of the book-sized journal, feeling the smooth tan leather on both the front and back covers. He opens it, and in reading through the tutorial pages, he comes to the first blank page. It is begging for pen strokes. Excited but nervous, he assesses his many possibilities of how to start writing. A colossal tower begins to form as the expectant moments pile up. *This must be what it is like to write the first sentence of a book.* He decides he should pray first, then determines that is what he is already trying to do with journaling.

Unsure why he has to try so hard, he just begins to write out his inner dialogue with this stranger, who goes by the name of God.

> Good morning God. Thank you for your blessings
> and love. Thank you for my family and thank you
> for my health. I'm sorry for the wrong that I do; I
> wish I could be better. Please forgive me.

After reviewing, he realizes he should have written in a much larger font to fill in the provided space, because he has nothing left to say after this.

I pray like a two-year-old child to a brick wall. How embarrassing.

He is thankful that nobody will ever see this journal except himself. Adan knows prayer is supposed to be a *conversation* with God, but he has never known or heard a prayer like that, much less participated in one.

The last prompt of the journal requires a reflection on the morning prayer. Looking out through the windows of his room which face the east, he admires the magnificent colors of the sunrise. Deep to light blue, orange to pink, then yellow to red with enormous snow-white clouds thoughtfully placed in the midst.

> Thank you for the sunrise. Give me a good day
> today. I love you.

Feeling unsure where the last sentence came from, he questions whether it is true. *Do I love God?* He doesn't really know what it is to love God, but he does know love, and if it's the same, then he lied. To

God. He continues to throw around the question as he finishes his tea, changes clothes, and heads to the gym.

The gym is usually packed. Mostly older people making feeble attempts to use every piece of equipment in the facility. Adan finds his corner empty and waiting for him. As he is stretching to warm up, a familiar face walks into the gym; before she notices him, he looks and admires her. Naomi is in a tank top and running shorts showing off her glowing, black skin. With her curly dark hair pulled into a bun, he realizes he has never noticed how beautiful she is, even with no makeup at 6:30 a.m. She sees him only a second before he says, "Wow. Look who came to the gym. Did you make a mid-year resolution to start working out?"

She looks at him with surprise. "Shut up. I run all the time, but the track was too busy, so I came here instead. What are you here for? Like showing off in front of all these old people?" she says with a cringe as a middle-aged woman walks past her with a scowl.

"Ha, no." He blushes. "I come here regularly. And I never compare myself to one of these old people."

"Hmm, with those flabby arms and legs, I seriously doubt that," she says.

"Yeah, okay. If these arms and legs are flabby, why can't you stop looking at them?"

Adan is wearing his cutoff shirt and gym shorts, but he finds himself with no advantage here as he is deeply intrigued by her voluptuous body, curvy and fit.

"I've just never seen them before, is all. You always wear a long sleeve button-up and pants to work, which I like seeing you in more," she says defensively.

Are we flirting with each other? Adan is undoubtedly attracted to her but is confident she doesn't feel the same. *She is just nice to everyone.*

"I'm sure you do. Did you know your face doesn't hide your lie very well?" he says as he takes a few steps backward, turning toward his preferred side of the gym to start his workout. Naomi mumbles something he can't decipher and makes her way to the treadmills.

At work, just over an hour after leaving the gym, Adan can't keep his mind off Naomi. *I can't believe I never realized how gorgeous she is.* He tries to convince himself to stop thinking about her since it is impossible she is interested in him.

Defeating his attempts to not think about her, she walks into his office, offering him the usual coffee, which he kindly declines. "Did you like class last night?" she asks.

"Yeah, actually, I did. I'm going to like the way Paul teaches for sure."

"Me too! I'm glad we're sitting next to each other; you'll always have the best answers."

"I don't know about always."

"I have no doubt you will. You should be the politician; they can pull the best answers out of their butt."

"That isn't much of a compliment; politicians suck, remember?"

"I didn't mean it as a compliment," she says with a smirk on her way out to offer everyone else coffee. He usually assumes as much, but today decides to peek. To his surprise, she walks directly back to the coffee maker, sitting it and the cup back in their place. Before she returns to her desk, she looks his way, catching Adan watching her, and smiles. He pulls his head back as fast as possible but it's too late.

By midday, Adan has already finished all work-related tasks and is deeply in thought about last night's meal at Paul and Lily's. He can't help but blush at how he fell apart so easily in front of them. The thing that is hard for Adan to believe, though, is that he doesn't feel exposed or in pain like he has always worried he would be if people found out he had issues. He is more confident today by admitting honestly how he felt about his relationship with God. *Paul and Lily are phenomenal people.*

As someone who grew up in church and believes in God, Adan never thought God was anything more than a judgmental figure who says he loves us and is our Father. The way Paul and Lily described Him, though, is like He is an actual person someone would enjoy being around. He is dynamic and alive in ways Adan had never thought possible. He found himself longing for what they had, a fulfilling relationship. He has never been entirely sure about what he wants or longs for in life until last night. Even with the pathetic attempt at a conversation with God this morning, he is still expectant for a relationship with Him. *I want to know God someday, like Paul and Lily do.* A grin takes over his face, sitting in his office alone at the feeling of something he hasn't felt in a long time. Hope.

Although he is still unsure how what Paul and Lily said about him could be true. *If I am a Christian, then I shouldn't have an addiction.* How could he be a good creation if he has an addiction? For the last seven years, he has worked hard to convince himself otherwise, but maybe it is something he could learn to accept.

Suddenly, he remembers what they said about attending church. For his entire life of doing so, not once has he been interested in knowing God personally. However, after only one evening with Paul and Lily, it's what is on his mind all day.

With so much to mentally process, he overlooks the time as it flies by, and 5:00 o'clock arrives quicker than expected. Before packing up for the day to leave, Naomi stops by his office again. Before he notices she is there, she asks, "Are you at the gym every morning?"

"Pretty much. Monday and Tuesday, and Thursday and Friday."

"Okay," she says.

"Why? Are you wanting to start coming more?"

"Not if you're there," she says, smiling.

"Rude." He can't help but be utterly confused by her. Typically, when they talk, she is friendly, but today she is being more sarcastic and somewhat mean, obviously messing around. He thinks for a moment that she might be trying to be flirtatious with him again but then shoots that thought down as he is convinced that's not possible. *She is way too pretty for me.*

"What are you doing tonight?" she asks.

"Going home."

"Wow, sounds lovely."

"It is. What about you?" he asks.

"Nothing yet," she says, letting the statement hang in the air. Unaware of the opportunity right in front of him, Adan pulls his backpack over his shoulder and says as he walks past her, "Sounds like a fun night. See you in the morning."

Before he pulls out of the parking lot, like a meteor slamming into earth, he realizes Naomi intentionally asked him what he was doing tonight and made sure he knew she had no plans. He puts the truck in park, jumps out, and runs to meet Naomi, who is almost now in her car.

What am I doing? What if she says no? Having no time to change his mind, he shouts, "Naomi! Wait!"

She looks over her shoulder, surprised to see him. "I thought you left?"

Out of breath, he asks, "Want to hang out tonight?"

At this, her face brightens with excitement. "Sure."

"I'm good with whatever you want to do," he says, trusting she had already thought of something.

"Do you like 'Game of Thrones?' I've wanted to re-watch it for a while now."

"Never seen it but sounds good."

"Okay, at my place?" she asks.

"I'm good with that; you live in the white house on Vine Street?"

"That's me!"

"Awesome. Do you like fajitas?"

"That's a stupid question." She laughs.

"You have a skillet and a stove, right?"

"I'm not a caveman."

"Okay! I'll buy some groceries and cook us dinner, too."

"Oh my gosh! Seriously?"

"Why not? See you in a few," he yells over his shoulder, running back to his truck, feeling her sweet eyes on his back.

That wasn't so bad.

At home, Adan changes into a T-shirt and a pair of his old running shorts, which are only two inches long.

This will make Naomi laugh.

On his way out, he stops in the living room to see his mom, who is on the phone. "See you later, Mom; I'm going to Naomi's; it shouldn't be later than ten when I get back," he says in a hushed tone trying not to interrupt her.

With big eyes, she looks at him. "Tiffany, I'll call you back in a bit." Then she directs her speech at Adan. "To whose house?"

"Naomi's."

"For what?" she asks with hopeful expectation.

"To eat dinner and watch a show."

"Yay! When did you plan this?"

"About 20 minutes ago. I asked her as we were leaving work."

"That's so sweet. Can't wait to hear all about it. Have fun! Oh, and she will love your cooking."

"I'll try," he says and walks out the door.

When pulling into Naomi's house, his nervousness returns. With groceries in hand to make his delicious fajitas, he walks up to her front door, and before he can knock, she opens it and gestures him inside. Once through the doorway, she says, "You showed up quick; it's not even six yet."

"What? Not used to seeing me show up somewhere on time?"

"Yeah, actually."

"Well, it does happen. Sometimes I even surprise myself when I show up on time," he says with a small laugh.

Naomi already has the skillet laid out when Adan unpacks the vegetables, tortillas, and steak. "So, you're a good cook, huh?" she asks.

"Who told you that?"

"Well, you must be pretty good to want to cook for a girl you're on a date with."

"This is a date?" he asks jokingly.

Her eyes widen. "What would you call this?"

After thinking about it for far longer than he needs to, he says, "A date." She slaps his arm and walks around to the other side of the bar. "I like your house. It's nice."

"Thank you. My dad helped me do some minor renovations," she says as she takes a seat, obviously intending to watch Adan as he cooks.

They spend the next hour visiting about work, college, and family. To Adan's surprise, she has five siblings. She couldn't wait to move out when she did last year and finally have a place of her own. "How did you survive with that many siblings? I have only one younger brother, enough to make me crazy."

"It was difficult, but I didn't know any different. I still see them and my parents a few times a week. I love them."

"It's true for me, too. My younger brother Ashby annoys me, but I love him."

Once the fajitas are finished, he warms up the tortillas then wraps them around the steak and peppers. Serving them on the plates, Naomi purposely made Adan search through all twenty cabinets and drawers. They take the food to the couch in front of her sixty-inch TV. "Dang, this is a comfortable couch," Adan says, sinking into the cushion.

"Glad you like it. Picked it up after searching all day through a furniture store. It was the only one that was pretty and comfortable. A rare find, apparently."

Naomi sits beside Adan, close enough for their legs to touch, as they attempt to eat without making a mess. *She even eats pretty.* He stopped himself from staring too long at her, but she caught a glimpse of him just before he pulled his eyes away. *I need to be quicker.*

"What?" she asks with her mouth full, reaching for the remote.

"Nothing."

"Were you admiring me?"

"Actually, yes," he says truthfully, not sure where to go with it.

"Never seen a girl eat like me before?"

"Actually, no." At this, she tips her head back with a laugh Adan can't help but join in on.

After their laugh, she turns the TV on and starts "Game of Thrones" season one. "You're going to love this," she says.

After watching two full-length episodes, during which Adan covered his face more times than he can count—and cheeks flushed so much he's not sure he will ever look normal again—Naomi turns the TV off. "So, did you like it?"

Despite the gore and nudity, he can honestly answer, "Yes."

"You don't like blood, do you?"

"No. Who would?"

"Yeah, me neither. You'll get used to it."

"I doubt I could get used to that. But the story and plot are fascinating, to say the least."

"Agreed," she adds.

They both flop along the couch like fish out of water in an attempt to overcome the cushions and sit facing each other. "So, you want to be a CPA with your own office, right?" Naomi asks with an agenda.

"Serious talk now, aye?"

"Yes. Now answer."

"That's the plan," he answers, intrigued.

"You don't seem very excited about it."

"I mean, it's a job and career goal. What is exciting about that?"

"Adan, you should pick a career you're excited about," she affirms.

"Nobody does that or can afford to anyway," he counters her.

"Sure, they do. Look at artists, authors, doctors, and teachers."

"You think the latter few are excited by their job? And the first two, those people are the lucky ones who make a living off their dreams."

"I'm sure some are, and you don't have to just be lucky to make a living from your dream, but passionate and good at what you do."

"Some and few," he chides.

"Then be a part of the few. Don't just do what our parents or culture says we should do," she continues.

"Okay, you're turning all motivational speaker on me now. What are your career plans?" He turns the question around on her.

"I don't know yet. I'm sure it's in the field of psychology, though. I still need to decide what I'm most excited and passionate about."

"So, you're still dreaming," he sings off.

"Yes. I think you should be, too."

Adan hasn't let himself dream about what he wants to do in life since he was a child when he thought anything was possible. He gets where Naomi is coming from, but understands life doesn't favor dreamers, instead the usual cultural standard. Any exception would be considered luck. "I'll consider that," he says to end that conversation. "Do you plan on leaving home after you graduate college?"

"Maybe," she says. "I'm honestly unsure. I don't like the idea of leaving my family."

"Same. I'm a big family guy." Suddenly he remembers Odell. "My older brother, my best friend, just moved away this week for a better job." "Odell?" she clarifies.

"Yeah."

"I'm sorry, that has to hurt," she offers.

"It definitely does." Careful not to cry in front of her. "I've seen how much it hurts my mom and dad, too, even though they are happy for him. I just can't do that to them."

"That's understandable. My parents would fall apart if I left. I stay because I love them, but not because I feel like I have to."

"I guess we are both the best children our parents could ask for," he says with a chuckle.

"Damn right we are," she adds with a laugh of her own.

By the time the clock shows 11:00, Adan feels like he has still only just arrived. They visit on the couch for almost two hours and could easily continue into the night. Knowing he needs to get back since it's an hour past when he initially said he would be home, he still finds it difficult to say goodbye. He looks at Naomi with a sense of familiarity but also like he has found a new and precious treasure. *She is beautiful in so many ways.* If he had more confidence, he would lean into her alluring lips and kiss her softly. "I better get home."

"Okay. It is way past your bedtime," she says with a smirk.

"That's right, I'm an early riser and need a solid eight hours of sleep."

"Well, hurry on home and get to bed," she says as they walk toward the door. Before he leaves, the tension in the room grows. *Should I hug her or kiss her on the cheek?* Settling on a hug, he leans over to her as she smiles, and they embrace for a moment. He pulls back, says goodnight, and heads home.

What happened tonight? That was the most comfortable date ever.

The evenings events replay for hours in his conscience, keeping him awake into the night. He has to convince himself multiple times: *It's not possible to fall in love with someone on the first date.*

SEVEN

One would think that after an entire week of trying to get to know someone, they would at least have more to say than they did the first time meeting them, that they would feel less awkward being around each other. That is not the case for Adan and God. Today marks seven full days of waking up 30 minutes earlier than usual just to make time to journal.

> Good morning again, God. Thank you for this day;
> I am grateful for it. Thank you for my family. I'm
> sorry for all that I do wrong; please forgive me. Give
> me a good day today. I love you.

Talking is much easier if the other person participates. He would admit, though, he enjoys journaling. The journal prompts are easy to follow and simple to finish. They give him a sense of accomplishment before the day even begins.

After wrapping up his futile attempt to have a conversation with God, his nose leads him into the kitchen at the smell of his mom's French toast. "Good morning, Adan," Renee greets him. "How did my boy sleep?"

"I slept well, Mom. Did you?"

"Same as usual. So, tell me about last night at Naomi's."

She has become especially interested in talking to Adan about Naomi since he first told her about her. He might call her nosey if she wasn't his favorite person in the world.

He has spent evenings at Naomi's house the last six days. One could call it a relationship now, but neither would say it out loud just yet. They are enjoying the casualness of it. "It was good, Mom; we just hung out and talked. Still getting to know each other."

"You describe it like it's boring. Give me more details, like what you talked about and how she looked at you."

"I love you, Mom, but that is all you're getting from me."

"Fine. When are you inviting her over for dinner?"

"Not sure. I'll let you know as soon as I do."

"Okay, I am excited to see you two together."

"Be patient, Mom."

"I can't. Just too happy for you. Anyway, I'm leaving for work; see you later tonight," she says with a huge grin.

Adan finishes his breakfast and cleans the kitchen as his dad walks in. "Are you going to Naomi's tonight again?"

"No, I have class, and Paul invited me to dinner at his house again."

"Okay," he says.

"Why do you ask?"

"Just wondering. Miss having you around in the evenings, but I'm happy for you, too." Seeing how this must be hard for his dad, he feels a bit of guilt. He is usually a homebody with a predictable evening routine. But his relationship with Naomi has turned his schedule upside down.

"Thanks, Dad. Love you," he says as he heads to work for the day.

Now that he and Naomi are seeing each other, work has become more enjoyable for Adan. Not that their small talk throughout the day has changed, but just being around her keeps things interesting. Adan even takes it upon himself to visit Naomi at her desk at least as often as she comes to his office. "What's up?" he asks as he walks to her desk pretending to need something from a cabinet.

Startled, she says, "Will you stop trying to find something? We both know you're here to talk to me."

"I've been found out," he says. "I'm going to ride with you to class today."

"Why?" she asks with a confused face.

"I want to know what riding up somewhere in such an attention-grabbing car is like."

"Whatever, my car is not *that* orange."

"Said the last guy, who is now blind from looking at it too long."

"Is that really the best you can come up with?"

He laughs, proud of his bad joke, and walks back into his office.

At class, almost half the people who were in attendance last week are gone. To Adan's surprise, they dropped the course. *Why would someone drop out of a class taught by Paul?*

When Paul finally makes it to class three minutes late, he carries a look of disappointment. "I guess I came off a little strong last week. Eight students dropped the class." The remaining students sit unsurprised. "They're going to miss out because tonight we are going to discuss some of the laws that affect us on a daily basis."

Adan spends the entire two-hour class period captivated by Paul's power to pull new insights from his mind. Unlike when a teacher tells the needed information, Paul's teaching method allows students to develop it themselves through a new lens. Much of what Paul talks about, people already know, but he brings it about from an entirely new perspective.

The evening's discussion topics range from seatbelt laws, speed limit laws, net neutrality, and tax laws. He comes to realize that most Americans are naive in their trust in the government.

Although the government is simply made up of other people, they can and regularly do test the boundaries of intrusion of people's rights.

He never knew he could be so interested in politics. He surprises Paul and Naomi with the startlingly accurate conclusions he draws long before the rest of the class even has a chance to finish hearing what all Paul has to say. His love for conversation is shown irrefutably by his new interest in a government and politics class, for which he previously had not one drop.

At the end of the lecture, the class becomes a busy highway as everyone offers one another goodnight farewells.

Disappointment weighs heavy inside Naomi's car as they pull into the office parking lot and she looks at Adan with sad eyes, asking, "Who is going to make me dinner tonight?"

"You have a ton of leftovers in your fridge," he answers, knowing what she means.

"Yeah, but I like it when you cook for me."

"Is that the only reason you like me?"

"Yes," she answers with her still sad eyes.

"You know, I'm not even surprised," he says, and both laugh together.

"I'm really going to miss you tonight, though. Seriously." She resumes her sad face features.

"Me too…" He finds himself with the perfect opportunity to land a kiss on her tempting lips, but still struggles to find the courage. So, he settles for just a side hug and exits the car.

"See you tomorrow!"

"Okay," she says, with a dispirited shrug.

On his way to Paul's house, excitement begins to simmer beneath his skin, as expectancy for an interesting conversation invade his mind. He has a full heart at the thought of his new friends, and although triple his age, he has no restraints from considering them as such. *A week is too long to be away from such exceptional people.*

The sunset is hanging over their little home with a splendor. It's like it has been photoshopped, with its perfection boasting itself. When he pulls in, he finds Lily tending to her garden on the south side of the house. He arrived before Paul only by a minute, and he can hear him pulling up the driveway.

"Evening, Lily." Adan smiles and waves.

"Adan dear. It's so good to see you again!" She carefully moves through the rows of tomatoes and squash over to him with a basket full of fresh produce. The aroma of earth and tomato plant attack Adan's nose as Lily wraps her arms around him in her signature hug. Today she is wearing a similar piece of clothing as the first time they met, only this gown has colorful fabric patches sewn on to cover up what Adan assumes to have been worn-out holes. "Could I show you around my gardens? Pizza is about to be in the oven."

"Sur-," he attempts to say, only to be met with Lily shouting over him instructions on how to cook the pizza to Paul, who has just parked.

"Will do, baby," Paul says, waving at Adan.

Lily takes Adan's arm and lets him lead her to where she directs.

They walk together throughout the many gardens. She explains why she planted the Garden Gerberas with Shasta Daisies, the Geraniums with Potato Vines, and many more combinations surrounding them. *This is an art to her.* The colors and scents surrounding them sparks multiple memories for Adan, those of past fascination with a variety of flowers and plants as a child. "I used to be filled with wonder at the smallest things."

"As we all are when we're children," she says with her voice of wisdom.

"I miss—most days—when my mind was that simple. Little to no worries whatsoever, only joy," he daydreams.

"Adan, a child's mind is anything but simple," she says.

"What do you mean? I think nothing like I did then, and I would like to think I am far more capable mentally now, too." *Or at least I think so.*

"That just means you've learned more and matured. It's a child's mind that leads them to learn, grow, and develop. Now, you reap the rewards of your younger mind's hard work."

"I've never thought of it that way, but that makes sense."

"As for your wonder at small things," she continues, "you've just chosen to appreciate the more complex parts of life. Which are fewer, but with being intentional, you can learn to let yourself be in awe of small things again too."

A part of Adan really would like to experience the joy of that again, not only because his mom would like it for him, but because he remembers how good it feels.

As Lily finishes their tour through her award-winning landscapes, she gestures for him to lead them to the back of the house. To his surprise, he finds a pergola with gentle lighting strewn throughout, built atop a brick floor, and Paul standing at the counter adding slices of pepperoni to a pizza. "Have a seat, Adan," Paul says. As he takes a seat, Lily meanders to the outside kitchen beside Paul to slice up her many vegetables and herbs.

"It smells divine," Adan exclaims. "And your backyard is just as breathtaking as the front." They have a small fire pit a few feet past the pergola and patio area where he is sitting, and more flower beds set against the backdrop of a small pine forest. The towering trees provide a majestic atmosphere to the outdoor space.

"Thank you. It is like our own world out here, just the way we like it." Paul and Lily don't strike Adan as the reclusive type, but they obviously enjoy their privacy and the room enough to express themselves.

Lily prepares a fresh garden salad, seasons the pizzas with fresh and dried herbs, and places them in their wood-fired pizza oven. Paul prepares the table with napkins, plates, and silverware. *They work together so well.*

During dinner, the trio discusses family, school, and a wide array of other things.

Conversation with Lily and Paul flows naturally and has a whole different level of familiarity for Adan now. Most would consider them new friends, but he feels he has known them forever. He is unsurprised when Paul pops the question, "So, how is your relationship with God?"

The temptation to lie and say "fine" is not as strong as it was the last time he was asked. "It's sort of an awkward monologue," Adan says.

Paul chuckles, as does Lily.

"That's normal," she says.

"I am a little disappointed, though, because I was hoping it would be like us talking here."

"Oh, Adan. Relationships with God take time. You can't expect to fall easily into conversation with someone until you've spent time with them and trust them," Paul explains.

"But I feel like I fall easily into conversation with you," Adan counters.

"Yes, very much so. But see, you still have little to no expectations of me. You can see me, and I talk back with an audible sound. You have endless expectations of God. Your perception of Him has been molded by your interpretation of other people's definitions. You must be willing to spend time with God, as awkward as it may be, and let your preconceived ideas be removed. Let God reveal Himself to you the way he wants to."

"Just by sitting and attempting a conversation?" Adan asks.

"Not only that; you must be intentional and honest. Ask God your questions; he isn't afraid of them. Open up about what's really on your heart. Talk to Him like you're talking to us now but have no expectations of what it should look like. Let the creativity and mystery of who God is be revealed to you."

"I really want that, but it feels out of reach," Adan admits.

"You're trying to *reach* too far. Take it day by day. Deepen your conversations a little more each morning; you'll be surprised by how far you'll come when you look back a month or a year from now."

"It would help if I could see Him. I don't have to hear him talk back but to see him…."

Paul responds, acknowledging Adan's dilemma. "Then ask Him to make Himself more present to you. Tell Him how you feel. Ask Him to teach you how to see and hear him."

Lily pipes in now. "When I talk to Jesus, He doesn't talk back to me in an audible voice, but through inspiration, comforting emotions, and tactile feelings. Communication reaches deeper than words. Sometimes even silence speaks more significantly than the most eloquently written prose. By talking to Jesus, you learn how to hone in on the original threads of communication.

Lily's response lights Adan's face up, and Paul adds, "God is *what* He is, not necessarily *who* he is. It helped me when I was still starting my relationship with God to call Him by name. It feels more personal and intimate."

"By name?" Adan asks. "Like being on a first-name basis?"

"Exactly."

That is odd. "What is His name?"

"Many different things. Throughout the Bible, you'll see him referred to by various unique names, my favorite of which is *Jirah.*"

"Jirah. That is a cool name." Adan lets the name live on his lips for a moment, taking it in. He loves the idea of knowing God on a first-name basis, but the impossibility of it towers over him. How could he, a young man addicted to pornography and self-gratification, ever come close to a place of knowing God? "I don't think I could ever be that close to God," Adan says.

"Why would you think that?" Paul asks.

"I know you said I'm a good creation, and I'm trying to believe that, but how can I know God well if I have an addiction? I claim to be a Christian and 'saved,' but I still struggle with it; I'm a hypocrite." Heat rises in him, red cheeks exposing his embarrassment, realizing he has just said far too much. *Not again.*

"Struggle with what?"

"I can't say."

"Can't or won't?"

"It's embarrassing," Adan says, putting up his best fight against his growing nausea.

"I can't help you with your question if you're not completely honest here, Adan."

Why is he pressing me so hard on this? As pushy as Paul is right now, he knows it's true. The power of pornography over his life is partly sourced from its secrecy.

"Pornography," Adan manages with a shaky voice. To his surprise, though, he doesn't burst into sobs, nor does the earth stop spinning, or the ground open to swallow him whole.

"I see," Paul says gently.

"I got saved when I was five or six. Since then, pornography has come into my life and won't go away," he admits.

"Can I admit something?" Paul asks, and Adan nods his head. "I've had an addiction, too." Paul's face remains strong. "I was a closet alcoholic for many years. I grew up in church the same as you and was saved at a young age. When I was in law school, I took up drinking." His face becomes strained. Adan glances and notices Lily's face streaming with tears as she places her hands on her husband's. "I struggled with that addiction for almost *30 years.*"

Adan is unsure what to say, dumbfounded by Paul's honesty, but it is encouraging. He cannot help but notice the lightness he feels in his chest, like helium pumped into a balloon; he could almost float.

"Adan, I was a saved man with an addiction. I didn't wait until my addiction was gone to start a relationship with Jirah. It was our *relationship* that helped me overcome it. If I were to have waited, I wouldn't be where I am today." He looks at Lily. "My marriage wouldn't be what it is today." He clears his throat. "Churches and many people teach and believe that sin separates us from God."

"But it does; that's what sin is," Adan questions.

"Is it? Find in the Bible where it says sin in any capacity separates us from God."

"I'll have to look it up."

"You won't find it anywhere. What you will find, though, is Romans Chapter 8, verses 38 and 39, which say, 'For I am persuaded, that neither death, nor life, nor angels, nor principalities, nor powers, nor things present, nor things to come, nor height, nor depth, nor any other creature shall be able to separate us from the love of God, which is in Christ Jesus our Lord.'"

"That is crazy to think about," Adan marvels.

"Jirah will meet you where you are now and walk beside you through your struggles, pain, and suffering."

"I want to believe this, but I've heard countless testimonies of people who had addictions, but when they got saved, their addictions left them. So, here I am, still struggling, even though I am saved. Does that mean I'm doing something wrong?"

Lily positions herself to face Adan again. "That's another thing the church teaches, that salvation is a moment, an epiphany-like experience that changes you forever." She speaks with fierceness. "Salvation is not a moment; it's a lifelong journey. Some people are blessed with having lost their addictions the moment they came to accept Christ, but the truth is the vast majority of people don't experience that. And that's okay."

"We have turned salvation into something marketable. We use tactics to 'bring people to Christ' by turning people's shame and guilt against them," Paul explains. "Salvation isn't even dependent upon us. It is for us and applicable to everyone. We don't have to accept salvation for it to be true, but we do have to accept it for it to change us, restore us, and redeem us, which happens through relationship."

"It sounds too good to be true, though," Adan acknowledges as he leans in toward Paul and Lily, allowing their words to fall on him.

"That is exactly right. What Jesus chose to do on the cross for us changed the world. We can enter into a relationship with Him personally and intimately. Knowing that our sole purpose in life is to love and be loved. To me, that sounds too good to be true, but it is nonetheless," Paul says with a thunderous and triumphant tone.

Adan just smiles and tries to get a solid grip on this incredible new understanding. "It'll take me a while to fully grasp this," he says.

"Honey," Lily says, "you'll spend your entire life trying but never fully grasp it."

He is grateful for these two people. The relationship he is building with them amazes him. "I don't know how I lived without you two before." He has never told a single soul about his addiction. Tonight was the first, and what he thought would leave him crippled and embarrassed has strengthened and empowered him through admission and honesty.

"We're glad to know you too, Adan. You are an extraordinary young man," they say, smiling. "Thank you. That means a lot," Adan responds. "And thank you for the delicious pizza!"

Adan helps clean up the table and kitchen. He does the dishes, Paul dries them, and Lily puts them in their places. She says Paul always messes up her cabinet organization, so she has grown accustomed to being the one who puts the dishes away. They sound like Adan's grandparents in that respect. Grandma is always on to Grandpa for doing something wrong in the kitchen, so she just takes over and does everything herself.

As he is washing the plates, a question circles in his mind begging to be asked. "Your lack of emphasis on our role in salvation has me wondering what it means to be saved, then, if salvation is given to us and we just need to accept it to experience it. Does that mean you believe everyone goes to heaven?" Adan is familiar with universalism and has always known it to be wrong, although it sounds like Paul and Lily might believe it.

Paul chooses to answer. "Our focus is on what Jesus did on the cross, which purchased the salvation of all mankind. Whether or not I believe it doesn't change the fact that it is true. Being saved often implies that we have to do something on our part to make it true when it is entirely Jesus who saves us. As for everyone going to heaven, let me ask you this. If our actions don't earn or bring us salvation, then how could they possibly withhold it from us? And if Jesus asks us to forgive those who trespass against us, even if they don't ask for forgiveness, then why would He not be willing to do the same?"

"So, my salvation isn't dependent upon me *asking* for forgiveness?"

"No. You don't hold the ability to limit salvation's reach."

"That is big. It makes sense because it is by Jesus' grace we have been saved, not by our own doing, but it's also against everything I have ever believed."

"Adan, I encourage you to read the Bible and ask Jirah your questions. Don't run to another person for answers because it will be saturated with their perspective but seek God's perspective. That is what Lily and I have done. You can come to understand the Bible better through a relationship with the one who inspired every word of it."

When the dishes are done, it's past 10:00 o'clock. Adan wants to stay longer but knows Paul and Lily are likely tired because even he is, and they are at least 40 years older than him. After thanking his gracious hosts again and giving hugs, he leaves for home.

Along the drive, past beliefs conflicting with new understanding are like the earth's tectonic plates, breaking the ground and exploding in the air. A mountain of purpose forms, as does a shout of excitement for the increasing hope that maybe his pornography addiction has an end in sight. Perhaps he really can have a relationship with God after all. Maybe he isn't a failure. If someone like Paul has had an addiction for half his life, Adan isn't too far gone. His heart is light, his joy overflowing. *I need to find a name for God!*

EIGHT

At Grandma's house for breakfast on Saturday, Adan is quizzed by Esme about his relationship with Naomi.

"When are we ever going to meet this beautiful, young woman?" she asks countless times while he is trying to eat his breakfast.

"Is she even real?" Ashby asks.

A cold and empty cavern moans inside of Adan as he sits with his family. The last week has been so busy with work, college, and Naomi that he hadn't said anything to Odell beyond a few short texts. He was supposed to come down for the weekend, but his team's first game is next Friday, so he decided to stay in Bolivar and sketch out a game strategy with his fellow coaches.

That promise to come home every other weekend sure lasted a long time.

Missing Odell doesn't last long for him when Grandma asks, "What are you doing today, Adan?"

"I'm hanging out with Naomi this afternoon; we're going on a picnic and a hike." "You can't stay away from that pretty girl, can you?" Grandpa interrupts.

"I guess not," he says, and Grandpa laughs.

A few minutes before noon, Adan pulls into Naomi's driveway. He wears a black shirt with his favorite pair of khaki hiking shorts. Adan made sandwiches and packed lunch for them. Naomi thought it would be best for him to do it, considering how he is "such a good cook."

He runs up to the door and knocks. "It's open," he hears from inside. He finds her on the couch in a bright pink tank top and black shorts, tying hiking boots that she has clearly never worn before.

"I won't have to worry about losing sight of you in the woods with that bright pink shirt," he jokes.

"And I won't have to worry about losing sight of you with those pale white legs," she shoots back without looking up.

"Pale?"

"A little tan, maybe," she says as she stands up and pulls her backpack over her shoulder.

"You're just jealous that your boyfriend looks better in shorts than you."

"Wow, cocky today, I see." She smirks. "Lunches ready?"

"Yep. With the best sandwiches you've ever had."

"Good, because I'm gonna be hungry," she says as the late morning sun greets them on their way out.

Along the way to McCormick Lake, a few miles out of Winona, in the middle of nowhere, Naomi and Adan find themselves debating whether country music is better than pop. Naomi wins, of course, so the playlist is hers to choose from, beginning with country songs from the 1980s. "I can't believe you like country," he mouths.

"I don't like it; I love it!" she corrects.

Wow.

When they turn off the main road onto the scenic drive into McCormick Lake Park, they both lean their heads forward and out the windows in a constant effort to get the best views of the picturesque trees and branches hanging over the road in a movie-like fashion. "I want to have a driveway like this one day," Naomi says in wonder.

"Definitely. It's so pretty that it looks fake," he says in similar awe.

"Imagine what it looks like in the fall when the leaves are changing colors!" she says. Adan can't resist the urge to watch Naomi as her hair wisps in the wind, her face glistening in the sunlight, and her eyes wide open, taking in the views before them. He has to jerk the truck back onto the road, having driven into the ditch from his distracted gaze.

"You're going ten miles an hour; how did you get us in the ditch?" she asks sarcastically.

"Saw something pretty," he responds.

Once they are at the lake parking lot, Adan grabs the cooler and Naomi the blankets. They find an area to enjoy right along the edge of the lake under the shade of a mighty oak tree. The scene is surreal, with no one around and the breeze playing in the leaves and stirring the lake's surface.

They talk and laugh about everything under the sun. Adan is always impressed by the fact that they never run out of things to talk about. Awkward silences are never *awkward* around her, just comfortable and quiet. It's obvious they are well-suited for one another.

They finish their lunch at a quick pace, as both are excited for the hike to the famed lookout spot that overlooks the Eleven-Point

River. It is a two-mile hike there, one way. Adan is grateful he wore comfortable hiking boots and for reminding Naomi to do the same.

After a few minutes into the hike, the trail guides them into the woods with trees and brush surrounding them on all sides, tickling their ankles with each step. "So, what do you do at Paul's house after class for dinner?" she asks.

A little taken aback at the question which came from nowhere, he answers, "Eat."

"I'm not stupid," she says flatly.

"Talk and eat," he jokes.

"I'm not scared to punch you," she threatens.

"Fine. We visit about our families and school, but mostly we talk about God," he concedes.

"Really?"

"Yep. He and his wife, Lily, are cool."

"Do you like talking about God?" she asks, still curious.

"The first time I went to their home, I didn't know them yet, so it was a little uncomfortable." *I'm not telling her I cried.* "But by the time I left that night, I had made two new best friends."

"That is really cool."

"It was. I've never met anyone like them before."

Naomi's face reveals her curiosity still stirring beneath her skin. "So, do you believe in God?"

Adan is surprised by the question then embarrassed by the fact that she even needs to ask him. He quickly answers, "Absolutely."

"I figured as much but still wanted to ask," she says.

"I don't do a good job of showing it yet, but I'm actually trying to build a relationship with Him and am learning to love Him."

Naomi smiles, obviously unsure what to say.

"I'm sorry I had yet to tell you; it's not something that comes up easily in a conversation," he explains.

"Oh no, that's okay. I'm glad you're telling me, though." She eases.

"So, do you believe in God?" he asks.

"I used to; I'm not so sure anymore."

"Why is that?"

"I am the oldest child in my family now, as you know, but I used to have an older brother, Chandler. He would be 30 this year, six years older than me." Adan can see her eyes swelling with tears as they continue hiking the trail. "He drowned when we still lived in Colorado," she says, stopping on the trail. She begins to let her tears fall. Adan gives in to his urge to hold her tight in his arms. "He took me swimming at the city pool when I was nine. He slipped off the diving board and hit his head on the ledge. No lifeguard was able to get to him in time before he was gone. I watched as they tried to resuscitate him for what felt like an eternity. He was only 15." She is weeping now, persuading Adan to hold her even tighter against his chest, massaging her back as she cries.

"I'm so sorry, Naomi. I'm so sorry," he comforts.

"I've hated God with a passion ever since. I don't understand why He would take my brother from my family and me like that. Why He would put us through so much pain."

"I understand where you're coming from. You are justified in the questions you ask."

"But he will never answer them," she says as she pulls back and wipes her eyes. "Thank you."

They resume their previous pace along the trail, crossing multiple streams of water along the way. Adan seeks out the best way across each, then leans back to hold Naomi's hand as she follows in his footsteps.

Nothing is spoken between them for a few trekking moments until Naomi says, "Sorry for coming apart back there; I didn't mean to put that on you."

I know what that is like. "You don't need to apologize."

As they continue on the path, they encounter dried-up creek beds, a common sight at the end of summer in the Ozarks. To complement the creek beds are huge mossy, green rocks jutting out of the ground and lush valleys full of wildflowers and mushrooms, all protected by the canopy of the ancient forest. Small animals like squirrels and chipmunks scurry all around them, reminders that they are in the midst of a diverse and fully alive ecosystem.

With one-quarter of a mile left to go, they come to a hillside that stretches upward farther than the eye can see. Naomi gives him a glance of hiker's regret, but Adan responds with a smile of reassurance, and so they begin their climb. "The view will be worth it," Adan encourages.

"Better be." She grunts as she forces another step.

The path is mostly clear, but tree roots and jagged stones clutter it every few steps, making the ascend much more technical. As they approach the top of the hill, the woods become more transparent, allowing further visibility. "We've made it!" Adan exclaims as he jogs past her to see the view.

The sun is resting flawlessly above the opposing hill, shining partly through the tree leaves, and its rays glistening off the currents of the river below. Rolling hills aggrandize before him, covered by thick forest growth, complementing the bend of the river, and working together in natural contours to spark wonder in the eyes of the beholder. "Wow..." Adan trails off.

"It was worth it," Naomi says with the sweetest voice. Adan glances at her, seeing a single tear cascade down her cheek, catching, and reflecting the sun. When she notices his gaze, he doesn't look away this time. They lock eyes. Her face is shining with rose gold and orange hues from the setting sun, clothing her like an angel. Adan doesn't question himself as he steps toward her, keeping his eyes on hers until they are less than an inch apart. He closes his eyes, leans into her, gently holding her chin with his hand, and places his lips on hers. His eyes might be closed now, but color explodes inside him. After a few moments, he lifts his head away, only to be pulled back down by Naomi's embrace to deepen their kiss. This time she is the one who pulls herself away with a smile brighter than the sun itself. Adan returns hers with one of his own, which makes him look like someone who just won a million dollars.

"I was beginning to wonder if you would ever kiss me," she says with a persistent grin.

"I've wanted to so many times!" He laughs.

"Why did you wait?"

"I guess I wanted it to be the most perfect, first kiss possible."

"Well, you nailed the timing!" she confirms.

"I'm glad. I like being with you in case I haven't said that yet."

"You hadn't, but I like being with you too."

They both laugh as they take a seat on the open hilltop. As they lay with their backs on the ground, Adan holds her in his arms, and they watch the sun finish its descent behind the trees. *I could get used to this.*

The hike back to the truck is a whole new experience. The darkness enfolds them as the sun's rays are no longer helpful for seeing where they are going. Even with the sun gone, the humidity and heat remain upon them as a comforting blanket. The darkness is sweetly broken up by the thousands of fireflies flying around them and their path, allowing curiosity and wonder to fill them.

"This is magical, Adan," she says as she spins in the presence of nature's splendor.

"I know! I could stay here forever," he says, sharing her tone.

"Can we?" she asks.

"Let's."

When they finally make it back to the parking lot, their eyes have fully adjusted to the darkness. Once out from under the trees, the moonlight exposes the path enough to turn off their phone flashlights and clamber inside the truck.

The drive out of McCormick Lake provides an entirely different view from before, with the moonlight filtered through the limbs hanging over the road. Neither says anything for a few minutes but just relax into their seats, preparing for the hour drive home. "That really was amazing today. I'm glad you brought me here," she says, admiring him.

"I agree, and you're more than welcome," he says, noticing a bit of tension flicker across her face now. "Naomi?" he asks.

"Yeah?" She looks at him again.

"You don't have to worry that I believe in God, and you're not sure whether or not you do. I'm not going to pressure you to believe one way or another. That is between you and God; I'll be here for you no matter what." His heart breaks as he sees her start to cry. He grabs her hand and squeezes gently.

"Thank you, Adan. You have no idea how much that means to me."

"Absolutely," he says.

"The way you talked about trying to know God better is foreign to me. I grew up believing people were either believers or unbelievers. Nothing about a relationship with God."

"That is me as well. I've gone to church my whole life, and I'm *only now* realizing I have never truly known who God is."

"So, how are you doing it? Getting or building a relationship with Him?" she asks.

"Well, I attempt to meet with Him every day, even on weekends. So far, I've done that pretty good. Now, I'm learning to be honest with Him about what I think and how to communicate deeper than words. Through presence and stillness. It sounds dumb when I say it out loud."

"No, it doesn't." She repositions herself to see him better. "It sounds like you really love Him."

"Really?" Adan could cry at the thought.

"No question. Love has to be involved to spend time with someone every day and give that much attention to detail."

Encouraged by her words, he decides to tell her more. "I'm trying out a new name for God."

"A new name?"

"Yeah, since God is *what* He is, not *who* He is."

"Okay, what is it then?"

"Abba."

NINE

Good morning, Abba. Thank you for today. I am excited to spend the day with my family and see Odell. Last night I struggled with pornography, but I can learn from it; I know what triggers my use. I feel disappointed in myself, like I'm dirty, but I know that is a lie, one I used to believe. Now, I know you have already forgiven me, and don't expect me to be perfect, but only to love you and be loved by you. Your presence is becoming so familiar to me that just being with you is encouraging. I love you, and I love spending this time with you. Naomi is coming over for dinner, and thank you for her, too, by the way! Tonight is the first time she will meet the entire family; please give us both some of your

peace and patience; we will need it. I can't wait for
the day that you have made! Love you, Abba.

After nearly a month of daily seeking Abba, Adan is finally feeling some level of growth. *Today I felt closer than ever!* Calling God by
name really does inspire intimacy between them.

He still doesn't hear God speak or see Him, of course, but in an
unexplainable way, he can feel His presence and His spirit enfold
him. His use of pornography has nearly halved, which he credits to
his growing relationship with Abba and his friendship with Paul and
Lily. They are still the only people to know about his addiction for
now. On the days he does succumb to the temptation to use porn,
he wakes up feeling the usual shame, but it is quickly removed by
the presence of Abba, who reminds him that he is on a journey, and
it takes a long time to overcome an addiction, especially one that
has plagued him for more than seven years. Understanding that salvation isn't a moment but a process, and that relationship requires
time, is difficult, but he grasps it a little more each day.

Since he moved, Odell is finally able to make it home on the
fourth weekend. He told Adan there was a surprise he was bringing
with him, and considering it is Odell, it could be anything, so he
doesn't spend too much time discerning what it might be. Adan has
yet to tell Odell about Naomi, so in a way, he has a surprise too.

Renee is the one who convinced Adan to invite Naomi over for
dinner; this way, she justifies Naomi can meet the entire family all
at once. His Mom hasn't considered their family whole since Odell
moved away, and this weekend she is the most excited he has seen
her in recent memory. Her eldest is visiting, and her middle child is
finally in a relationship.

Adan has graciously offered to help his mom cook an enormous
meal. Counting grandparents, they will be cooking for almost ten

people. Mom is sparing no expense on the dinner course, either. Chef salad for an appetizer, sweet dinner rolls, steak, cheesy fried potatoes, and BBQ beans as the main course. To complete the meal, she is concocting a cherry cheesecake, which is Odell's favorite, and a peach cobbler, which is Adan's. She sends him to the grocery store with a mile-long list, culminating with enough groceries to stock the kitchen for months.

Adan is not proud of his poor grocery-shopping abilities. For a few items, he is suitable for it, but send him to the store with a list of this size, and he crumbles. So, he enlists his Grandma Esme's help. *She knows where everything in the store is at.* He pulls into her driveway, finding her already standing outside waiting for him. "You know I'm never early, Grandma." He apologizes.

"One can only hope," she says while pulling the seatbelt around herself.

"I'm 20, Grandma. No hope for me."

"Wow, you must think I am a sorry old lady stuck in her ways."

"No, not even close." Adan gives her an affectionate look.

"You're never too old to change and make better choices," she lectures.

"That's true. I need to be on time more often," he admits.

Ignoring what he says, she continues to ask, "So, this girl, Naomi. We're meeting tonight. Are you two serious? Do you really think she could be the one?"

"Slow down, Grandma, she's just coming for dinner; this isn't an evening to plan a wedding."

"I know, but you need to think about those things now, not later."

"I do like being around her, and I see no reason yet why it wouldn't last." "Good. Very good."

It never ceases to impress him the depth of conversation he and his grandma are able to squeeze into the five-minute drive to town. Upon walking into the store, they are met with multiple familiar and friendly faces, including Lisa, their family friend. They make time for quick small talk, an unspoken expectation of living in a small town.

Once inside, Grandma takes Adan's list, charges him with finding items on the opposite side of the store, and instructs him on the approximate location of each one. "I don't know what I would do without you, Grandma."

"You'd be here into the night and still not find everything," she teases.

That is precisely what would happen.

After loading a shopping cart to its brim with meat, vegetables, and beverages, they make their way through the lengthy Saturday-morning checkout line and load the groceries into his truck.

Along the short drive home, they partake in the energy and excitement they both share that Odell is coming home.

"My heart will be so full today," she exclaims. He can see her joy, emulating his mom's, exuding from every part of her. He can't help but smile inside and out. *My family is the best!*

After dropping his grandma off at her house, he pulls into his own driveway and is greeted by his dad pulling out the wood pellet grill for what will soon be cooking the steaks to perfection.

"Need help?" he asks Adan, assuming his stumbling legs cannot support two arms overloaded with grocery bags.

"No, I got it. Thank you, though," he says confidently.

"You know, your legs will carry you through more than one trip of groceries."

"Nope," he says as he plows his way into the house, kicking the door shut behind him while teetering on one leg.

Out of breath, he unpacks all the groceries that his mom requested he buy; they completely cover the kitchen island. "Got everything?" His Mom asks from behind as she walks into the kitchen.

"Lord, I hope so."

She only smiles back and rolls her eyes.

"Do you know what Odell's surprise is?" he asks, assuming she might know.

Confirming his suspicions, she answers without looking at him, "I do."

"And?"

"You'll find out soon enough."

"Really, you're not going to tell me?"

"Nope. You'll think it's both ironic and funny, though."

"That could be anything."

"It wasn't a hint."

"You're no fun at all, Mom." He surrenders his attempt to pull information from her.

"Put your apron on and help me get started," she demands.

"On it." He pulls out the colorful apron he made himself when he was eight years old.

"Still looks good on you." She sings as he straps it around himself. "Good thing you haven't got fat yet."

"Yet?"

"If your dad and grandpa are any indications…"

"That isn't always how it works." She only looks at him with unconfident eyes and a raised brow. "Is it?"

"We'll just have to see," she says. "Now, start chopping the lettuce."

While preparing dinner, the doorbell rings.

"It's open!" Mom yells, but the guest at the door only continues to ring the doorbell repeatedly. "Will you just go get that, Adan?" Renee asks, annoyed.

"On my way." He finishes chopping the last carrot, then waltzes to the door. He notices Odell's face in the window before opening it, his excitement quickly removed at the sight of his brother with a woman—who is likely Odell's age—hanging from his arm. *Oh no.*

"Adan!" Odell exclaims, latching on to him and pulling him in for a bear hug. "I've missed you, man."

"Back at you." Adan forces his best smile despite the awkward surprise. *Mom wasn't kidding when she said "ironic."*

"I'm sure you have guessed my surprise by now. This beautiful woman is Amira." Amira is tall, almost as tall as Odell, and effortlessly beautiful. She has long, golden brown hair and a dimpled smile. Adan stretches out his hand as they greet each other.

"Nice to meet you, Amira. What a charming name!"

"Thank you." She laughs nervously. "It was my grandmother's."

Adan steps back to allow his brother and girlfriend to pass by and into the kitchen. It is then he realizes he is still wearing his colorful children's apron and quickly unties and pulls it off.

Amira notices, "Did you make that recently? I love the colorful unicorn."

Smart aleck. You'll be perfect for Odell.

"Yeah, a few days ago. Worked hard on it," he says, making her chuckle. Her shoulders hunch slightly, and her eyes are all over the room as she follows in Odell's footsteps.

Adan's heart melts when he sees his mom dote over Odell when he comes into her view. She embraces him with tears flooding her cheeks. "Mom, meet Amira, the girl I've told you so much about." Amira's cheeks blush, and Mom can tell she's nervous too. Renee saves her hugs for only extraordinary occasions and has decided to spend two in one greeting when she wraps her arms around Amira.

"It's nice to meet you, Amira; you are even more beautiful than Odell could have described, and he already had me convinced you were the most beautiful girl in the world," Mom says as she releases the hug, and Odell's face shines pink with a hint of embarrassment.

"Thank you, Renee. It's nice to meet you, too," she says with a quiet voice.

"Did you already see your dad?" Mom tears her attention back to Odell.

"Yeah, before we came in."

"Good, you can stay in here with me."

After Odell and Amira sit down at the bar to snack on chips and guacamole, Renee conducts her interview of Amira, not as sly as she thinks. Amira is aware of what Mom is doing but plays along as she asks questions ranging from where she and Odell met to their future. Amira's face couldn't turn redder without exploding. Unsurprisingly she asks, "Where is the restroom?" Odell points her in its direction.

"Mom, you're making her nervous," Odell complains when Amira is out of earshot.

"Whoops," she says, pretending to be aloof.

"Mom, you know exactly what you're doing…" Odell whines.

"Fine, yes. Sorry, Odell, you know I can't help but ask endless questions. I'm so happy for you. And I want to make sure she is good enough for you," she apologizes.

It is clear she has not told Odell anything about Naomi yet, which makes Adan happy to be able to surprise him. *He just thought he had me by surprise.* "So, how is the Bolivar life treating you?" he asks.

"No words. It's better than I dreamed it would be. The people and the athletes are all just simply amazing."

Adan is embarrassed by himself as he realizes he inwardly wants Odell to be unhappy since he left. Hoping that his unhappiness would make him move back. Dismissing his selfishness, he says truthfully now, "That is amazing! I am so glad for you."

"Thank you. How are work and school going for you?" Odell asks.

"Work is the same. College is surprisingly excellent this year; the seated class is incredible with an extraordinary professor."

"Who is becoming a good friend of yours, too," Mom pipes in.

"Yeah, he has invited me to dinner with him and his wife every week since classes started. He and his wife are becoming my closest friends."

At this last comment, Odell glances downward. "That's interesting; I'm glad you've met some good people." Adan quickly changes the subject. "Want to go and sit outside on the patio? I'll grab a couple glasses of tea."

"That sounds great!" he says.

"So, you're leaving me alone?" Mom says pitifully.

"No, we're just giving you space to get to know Amira. Don't scare her away, though," Odell says.

"Can't promise you anything," she smirks, likely contemplating a multitude more questions to ask poor Amira.

Outside on the patio, old habits resurface as Adan jabs. "Mom might tell Amira some old stories about you."

"Oh, I'm not worried. She's too shy to pull any of the good stories out of Mom." Odell responds, not returning Adan's comment with one of his own.

The two talk for over an hour on the patio. Topics range from the most exciting events in the last month to how much they've missed each other. The latter of which brings forth an apology from Odell.

"I've seriously missed you this month, man; I didn't realize how much I need your company. I'm sorry I left home so quickly."

The level of growth in Adan's faith and character is shown in his quick response. "It's ok. I'm not mad anymore and am sorry for how I acted. I took your advice and have let some people into my life. It's changed everything for me. I even have a new and growing relationship with God, whom I call Abba. It's the coolest thing." *Still sounds weird saying it out loud.*

"You're something else, Adan. You have no idea how good it makes me feel to see you like this," Odell says, clearly at peace now. Adan just smiles back at his brother. "You better get back inside to make sure Amira is ok."

"Oh yeah! You're right!" Odell says, almost forgetting about her. "But actually, first, what do you think of her?"

"I think she is stunning and seems genuinely nice," Adan says honestly.

"Good. I can't wait for you to get to know her better; you'll like her a lot. She means the world to me."

As Odell steps back inside, Adan reads a text from Naomi letting him know she is on her way. His grandparents have pulled into the driveway and are walking to the front door, which Adan gladly runs to open for them. Dad is following them in with a tray full of juicy steaks. "Thank you," each says as they walk by him.

Inside, Mom and Amira have finished setting the table and are loading it with the food ready to be served.

"Where is Naomi?" Grandma shouts at Adan from across the dining room into the kitchen. "She is on her way," Adan explains.

"Who is Naomi?" Odell asks, confused, of everyone in the room. When nobody answers, he looks at Adan with widening eyes, and his entire face shouts excitement. "You have a girlfriend?" he asks as he walks over to Adan and slaps his back.

"She is special; I'm excited for you to meet her!"

"Me too," he says.

"We all are," Mom interjects.

"Oh, so nobody has met her? Even better!"

The doorbell rings just after everyone finds their seats at the table full of scrumptious food. *This is it.* "I'll get it," Adan says.

"She is here," Grandma Esme says with delight as she rubs her hands together like an excited kid. When Adan opens the door, he silently gasps at the sight of Naomi standing before him with her simple yet breathtaking beauty. She is wearing a sophisticated white shirt studded with a few subtle rhinestones, jeans, bold earrings, and necklaces, and her curly hair is flowing as vibrant as ever.

"You look beautiful," he whispers.

"Thank you," she mouths back.

As if purposely opposite Amira, Naomi walks into the dining room with a confident posture, an audacious smile, and eyes trained on each person she is about to meet. Adan has a sense of pride fill up inside him. *She is brilliant.*

After a few short introductions, handshakes, and hugs, Naomi can take a seat beside Adan. As the family joins together in inclusive discussion, they learn that Amira is a full-time nurse practitioner. She and Odell met through friends and hit it off well, surprising both of them. Odell has found an apartment of his own now and will need help in the coming weeks to move his belongings—which Adan offers himself kindly. The family also learns about Naomi's ambitions as a college student, still unsure about what kind of career she wants long-term, but knows it is somewhere in psychology.

The scents of homemade food and the warmth of family seated closely wrap around him like a blanket of fullness, Adan's heart acknowledges his contentment in this moment. The conversations rest in the background as his mind clears and he expresses his innermost gratitude. *Thank you, Abba, I love you.*

After most everyone's sides hurt from laughing during the long, eventful meal, Grandma and Grandpa call it an evening and head home. Ashby makes his way downstairs to indulge in his favorite video games. Odell and Amira have found themselves in each other's private company on the patio. David also steps out of the dining room to find his chair in the living room to watch the Andy Griffith Show, leaving Naomi, Adan, and Renee at the table together. Renee's eyes betray her—this is the moment she has been waiting for—giving Naomi a moment to prepare. "So, Naomi," she says with a quizzing tone. "What's your family like?"

Here come the questions.

Naomi ponders her answer for a moment, carefully planning her response. "Well, we are a family of adventurers, always on the move and ready for a challenge. We also stick together through everything; nobody is left to live life alone in the Moore family."

"That is sweet," Mom says softly.

"They are an intense bunch of people," Naomi continues with a laugh. "I've had my own home for over a year now, and it's been so nice to have a place of privacy outside my family, but I am still close enough to see and spend time with them almost every day."

"I see. Family is obviously important to you."

"More than you know," she says.

Mom squints her eyes, trying to read Naomi but apparently having difficulty. She moves her gaze to Adan. "Adan, go sit with your dad for a moment."

Unwilling to disobey his protective Mother, he gives a look of reassurance to Naomi, who shows no sign of fear. "You've got this," he whispers. Naomi keeps her gaze fixed entirely upon Renee. Adan stands up and walks from the table into the living room with his dad.

"Mom interrogating Naomi?"

"Yep."

"Hope she has tough skin."

"Me too."

After finishing almost two full episodes of the Andy Griffith Show, laughter invades the living room as Renee and Naomi appear.

That's a good sign.

"Ready to leave?" Adan asks Naomi.

"Yep," she confirms and gives Renee a big hug.

Mom has spent an entire year's worth of hugs in one day.

At her car, Adan asks, "So Mom didn't scare you too bad, right?"

"Not at all," she chuckles. "She is easily the nicest person I've ever met." Adan's chest becomes warm, and he relaxes with a slowed heartbeat. *She likes Mom.*

"I'm so glad you like her. I'm sure she will never stop talking about you now," he says, and Naomi just grins.

"You owe me now, though," she says.

"What do you mean?"

"I met your entire family; now you have to meet mine."

"I'll accept that. I'm excited to meet the people who helped craft your personality."

"Good, hold on to that excitement; they can be scary people," she says as she sits in her car. "I'm not worried. Anyway, have a safe drive home." He drops his head down to meet hers with a kiss. "Talk to you tomorrow."

"Thanks," she says with a big smile. Adan shuts her car door and waves as she drives away.

He climbs the steps back into his house and walks inside to find his mom, who is sitting in her usual spot, beaming from head to toe. He assumes his dad has already gone to bed and takes his seat. "So, what did you think?" Adan asks.

"It was a nice dinner. Thank you for your help," she says.

"About Naomi?" He gives her a dramatic sigh.

"Oh, you mean the angel that just left?"

"If that is how you describe her, then yes." He can't help but smile obnoxiously at his mom's opinion of her.

"Adan." She leans forward. "She's gorgeous, and her personality is richer than gold. I only just met her, but you know I'm a good judge of character."

"I'm glad you like her."

"You two are hardly anything alike, but I think that is why you get along so well."

"I know, me too! Opposites attract isn't just a saying; it's proven quite true." He can't help but ask, "What do you think of Amira?"

"She is sweeter than honey, albeit shy and nervous, but lovely."

"I agree; she seems down to earth."

"Back to you and Naomi, though. What are your plans there?" Mom retakes the conversation, now leaning over the arm of the couch.

"Mom, we've only been dating for one month."

"So?" she says.

Adan can't deny the feeling he has inside now that he knows his mom likes Naomi and vice versa. He can confidently answer his mom, saying, "I think I want to marry her."

TEN

ONE YEAR LATER

I t doesn't take long to become a professional at hanging rope and stringing lights when you can do so dangling from a tree limb. Adan looks like a sloth as he stretches across the enormous limb of a magnificent oak tree, wrapping white rope lights around it. Laser-focused, he finishes one limb and climbs to the next; he has also enlisted Ashby's help. His position involves unboxing and untying the lights and handing them to Adan. They have successfully wrapped four oak trees and ten pine trees with white rope lights—trunks, limbs, branches, and all.

After stapling the last stretch of lights to the tree, Adan climbs carefully back down and gazes up at his work. "I can't wait to light it up," he brags.

"Me either," Ashby says. He is 17, and the two have come a long way after one year; they worked together ably, preparing a serene place in the woods for Adan to propose to Naomi. "We are all out of lights."

"Good, 14 trees lit up at night will be dramatic enough."

"I agree."

"Now we just have to hang the string lights from overhead, connecting tree to tree," Adan says.

"Seriously? You want to have lights strung overhead, too?"

"Yeah, why not?"

"Fine. We've done this much; surely, we can do a few more."

"That's the spirit!" Adan exclaims. His plan is to set up a rustic dining table amid the lights and trees, with bouquets of flowers dropped all over the ground contrasting the brown leaves of the forest floor.

Naomi is unlike anyone else in the world to Adan, so she deserves the most unique and elegant proposal. The part of the night's itinerary he likes best is that they will eat dinner at the single dining table in the woods under the lights and stars. After proposing, their family will arrive and congratulate them, joining in a cacophony of praise and excitement for the blessing and love of Abba.

If all goes according to plan, tears will be shed, and Naomi and Adan will be engaged. Adan can't take all the credit for the incredible idea; it was inspired mainly by his mom, who then helped carve out an actual scheme for an event like this.

Three months ago, Adan became sure he wanted to marry Naomi. After nearly nine months, he committed.

Adan asked his mom one morning. "Mom?"

"Yes, dear," she acknowledged.

"I'm going to ask Naomi to marry me," he said casually.

Renee's face lit up. "Oh my gosh, finally!"

"We've been together for one full year Mom; it's a fair amount of time to give a relationship."

"Is that all it's been? Seems like you two have been together forever."

"Of course, you think that, Mom. In your mind, I should have already been married." He laughed.

"How are you going to do it?"

"Well, I need your help. I want it to be like nothing she could expect but also simple and comfortable."

"Okay," she said, deeply in thought.

"I want our families all there after I have proposed, and she says 'yes'. Only after that can everyone celebrate."

Mom rolled her eyes at him. "She is going to say 'yes'."

"But *just* in case she doesn't, I don't want everyone already there celebrating; it would be the most awkward moment of my life put on a stage for all to see."

"I see. I'll devise something, and we'll figure it out."

Over the next couple of months, they threw ideas at each other, most of them rejected, except when Adan heard his mom's idea of a picturesque dinner with a colorful backdrop against the woods. Something about that one struck a chord. From there, they drafted the plan to do it at night and chose how many lights to hang literally everywhere possible. After spending a few hundred dollars on lights, it was time to start working on hanging them and preparing the place full of expectation. Over four weeks, they picked the spot on the family farm and began clearing out the area and a trail to get there.

"Are you nervous?" Ashby asks.

"No, I don't think so."

"I would be."

"Why?" he asks, genuinely interested now.

"Because it's perfect out here, and you love her...It would be a lot to handle."

"You're right, but it feels natural. We've done all this," Adan gestures to the lights and table. "Just for dramatic effect. She would be okay with me proposing on a sidewalk somewhere, too." Ashby says nothing more, but Adan adds, "Thank you so much for your help. Couldn't have done this without you."

"You're welcome. What time are we supposed to be here?"

"I'm picking her up at 7 p.m.; it should be dark by then. Everyone needs to be here by 8 p.m. awaiting my text for the all-clear to walk down here and celebrate."

"Okay, sounds fun. I'm going home; see you tonight."

"Okay, thanks again!" As Ashby heads to the truck to leave, ruffling leaves announce Renee's presence.

"I'm making chicken parmesan and salad with Italian dressing for your meal tonight. Then I have a peach cobbler and apple pie I'll bring for everyone afterward."

"Sounds amazing!"

"Naomi is the luckiest girl in the world." She looks at him with all-consuming loveliness, and her tears sparkle as they fall from her eyes. "I'm so happy for you, Adan."

Seeing his mom cry makes his eyes burn until he lets his own tears fall. "I love you, Mom. Tonight is going to be perfect because of your help. I'm the luckiest son in the world," he says as they embrace one another.

6:45 p.m. comes quickly as Adan finishes his shower and changes into a simple black dress shirt and khaki-colored jeans. He texts Naomi to let her know he is on his way.

Along the drive, he ponders the extent of what has changed in his life.

His relationship with Naomi has evolved from that first casual date they had, which feels like only yesterday. They are now both ready to make lifelong commitments to each other. Around this time last year, he had such low self-confidence. He had never been in a genuine relationship and was painstakingly unsatisfied with his life. Now though he is excited to wake up in the mornings, he is in love, not only with Naomi but also his Abba. A relationship with God has enriched his life and every other relationship he has. His struggle with porn has been nearly eradicated now that he goes to sleep content in himself at night. He has learned that speaking with Abba is more about being present in the moment than saying something. Silence is the stage upon which his true self speaks.

Even though Adan's American Government class is over and has been since last year, he still joins them both for dinner every week. They have truly become family. Naomi joins their dinners now, too, and Paul and Lily carefully respect her fragile belief in God. They have been an example to Adan and Naomi of how wonderful a marriage can be.

To think, the moment Odell left for Bolivar—which initially caused Adan to be angry at the loss of his best friend—was the catapult that helped him be brave with Naomi and allow Paul and Lily into his life. They inspired him to have a relationship with God in a way he never thought possible. *I'm not even the same person anymore; I'm content and happy.* Sadly, such feelings can be stripped away so quickly.

When Adan makes it to Naomi's house and parks the truck, he collects his thoughts and focuses on acting as normal as possible. He is sure she will figure out the events of the night before the actual moment of proposal, but he doesn't want his fidgeting and excitement to give it away.

A moment after he knocks on the door, Naomi pulls it open to reveal herself dressed in a visually stunning yellow sundress. "Wow, you look *ravishing* this evening."

"*Ravishing*, really? Pull that one out of your butt?"

"Just complimenting you on your sophisticated beauty."

"Thank you. You look good, too," she admits.

"Good?" he asks, disappointed.

"Hot. As you always do."

"Wow." He blushes. "Thanks."

"Don't let it go to your head."

"Understood."

After they are in the truck and on their way to the outdoor venue he has specially created for this evening, Naomi asks, "So where are we going?"

"Somewhere remarkable."

"Just tell me." She throws her head to the side and glares at him.

"It's only a minute's drive."

The scene awaiting them is only accessible by driving through a field. Naomi casts a confused look as they navigate through the gate along a temporary gravel driveway with lush green grass on both sides.

"Seriously, though, why are we driving through a field? You said we were on a date. Usually, that involves a restaurant and food."

"I didn't lie," Adan says with confidence. Naomi just shakes her head with annoyance.

Renee timed her food delivery perfectly because they are the only ones there when they pull up to the wooded area. He parks the truck, jumps out, and gracefully helps Naomi onto the grassy ground below. The sun is now completely set, and the sky is decorated with stars and galaxies. Adan leads her in the direction of the path through the woods, but before they are on their way, she pulls away from him.

"Tell me what's going on. I'm freaking out, and you're acting like everything is normal; this is not normal!"

Adan calmly faces her and smiles reassuringly. "It is still a surprise; I won't let anything in the woods hurt you, I promise."

"If something scares me, you will be the one needing protection, *from me*. I'll kill you, and I mean it," she says with both a convincing tone and a face of steel.

"Deal."

"I'm going to die tonight," she says in the empty air as she folds her arm around Adan again, and they begin their short journey into the woods. The table is set up less than 400 meters from the edge of the woods, just so that when all the family parks, they won't be a distraction.

Adan stops at the point where the battery-powered generator is sitting. As he lets go of Naomi for a moment to turn it on, he says, "Close your eyes."

Naomi's voice squeaks, "I'm scared." And she covers her eyes.

"Don't be," he says and turns it on.

Like an explosion, the area before them bursts to life with a forcefulness of grandeur. Thousands of individual lights work harmoniously to light up entire trees and their neighbors' silhouettes. The overhead lights create softness and comfort in the air. The table and two chairs are the last pieces that come into focus with their simple charm.

"You can move your hands now," Adan advises.

Naomi gazes at the scene showing off before them, the boldness of beauty causing her jaw to drop. Her eyes reflect the colorful lights around them, mesmerizing Adan as he watches her reaction.

"Oh. My. Gosh," she exclaims. "Is this real?" To add to the drama already in motion, Adan draws her attention to the firefly light jars hanging without order throughout, reminding them of the night of their first kiss. "This can't be real." She spins around, taking it all in.

"It is." As Naomi begins to cry, he says, "You can't cry yet."

"Yet?" she manages. "Are you going to—"

"Let's just eat dinner, shall we?" He cuts her off, and they walk towards the table set perfectly with plates and silverware. She wipes her eyes and smiles genuinely as she takes the seat Adan pulls back for her.

He unpacks the hidden cooler full of food his mom has prepared. He then places the serving dishes, revealing an aromatic and excellent Italian dinner. He sets tongs and serving utensils on the table and serves himself and Naomi the salad and chicken. Before he sits down to eat, he remembers the music. He runs back to the generator a few feet away, plugs in the speaker, and picks a jazz playlist from his phone.

"Jazz, really?" she asks with a side-bent grim.

"I know, I know. I don't like jazz either, but it seems to suit tonight's theme."

"It really does. Thank you." She nods in agreement.

The two of them enjoy their food, sitting under the starry night sky in a dream-like atmosphere, protected by the majestic, brightly lit oak and pine trees, only exaggerated by the expectancy that fills them.

Once they finish eating, Adan reaches across the table to take Naomi's hand in his. "I'm sure you already concluded why we are out here, but I still have something to say." Adan pulls from his mind the memorized lines he has been creating for the last few weeks. She looks deep into his eyes as he speaks. "Naomi, you are my best friend. You keep me smiling and laughing all the time. You keep me accountable and authentic to who I am. You inspire me to be the best man I can be. It's easy for me to be me when I'm with you. Your heart is more beautiful than pure gold, and your eyes more captivating than an evening sunset. Everything in me screams that you are who I was made to be with. I want to wake up every day to your gorgeous face and tell you how much I love you, because I do, Naomi; I love you." Adan is crying now, and Naomi started before he even began talking. He drops to one knee beside her and asks, "Naomi Moore, will you marry me?" He holds his breath.

"Yes! Of course!" she screams, jumping onto him, and they kiss and tumble to the ground, holding each other tight. "I will marry you, Adan Caddell."

After Naomi and Adan pick themselves off the ground from lying on their backs and stargazing through the canopy of leaves above, he remembers to text his mom and let her know they are safe to come. After only a moment from sending the text, Renee, David, Ashby, Odell and Amira, Grandma and Grandpa, Naomi's parents, and four brothers all come barreling through the trees like a mad bunch of people. Renee screams gleefully as she pulls both Naomi and Adan into a hug.

"I'm so happy for you two!" she exclaims as she steps back to let everyone else have a turn at hugs and congratulations.

Odell carries in plastic plates and silverware, while Ashby carries in the apple pie and peach cobbler. The group indulges in fellowship and dessert, sharing a in a feeling of enthusiasm for the new engagement.

As Adan holds fast to Naomi, both with unfading smiles powered by tremendous joy and being surrounded by the family he
loves so dearly, he finds himself with everything he could ever want.
Unbeknownst to him, the feeling would soon be a distant memory.

ELEVEN

The smell of yeast and cinnamon fills the warm air in Naomi's house. Adan spends the afternoon teaching her how to make cinnamon rolls. They both took off work early to prepare dinner for themselves and Paul and Lily. Adan still works as an accountant for Lester and Associates, but Naomi took a new position recently as a high school counselor. After three weeks into the new job, she absolutely adores it. She has finally found her "calling", as she puts it.

Teenagers whose emotional struggles are often overlooked or dismissed as something they will simply outgrow found a place in her heart. She continues to push Adan into going after what he really wants in a career, what he dreams of doing. If he is honest, though, he has come to be content where he is. It isn't talked about enough, but if someone is satisfied at home and within themselves, it will carry over into their work. A few career options pique his interest, but for now, he is enjoying watching Naomi go after her dream.

They have picked a date for their wedding, December 10th, 2021. It is close to his mom's birthday, not purposely, but Renee is convinced it is the best gift ever. At least Adan won't have to find anything else for her birthday this year. Adan and Naomi both prefer the idea of an intimate and straightforward wedding over a lavish and showy one so they can save money for an incredible two-week honeymoon in Tahiti. His family has already had the opportunity to be a part of an enormous wedding this year, with Odell and Amira's being nothing less than extravagant. It was beautiful and memorable. Over 200 people showed up. Although show- stopping, it confirms Adan and Naomi's plan for a low-key service.

"You'll want to take your ring off before we knead the dough," Adan says.

"Right, don't want it to get lost in a cinnamon roll," she says as she slides it off slowly.

Adding flour in dashes to keep the dough from sticking to their hands, the child in each of them comes out in accidental tossing of flour to the face. When the dough is ready to let rise over the warm oven before baking, each looks like the Pillsbury Doughboy.

They had contemplated the idea of Adan moving in with Naomi now that they are engaged; however, considering their families' Christian conservative viewpoint, they quickly determined it would cause more fuss and headache than it was worth. Waiting until they were legally married to live together didn't seem so bad.

At precisely 6:00 o'clock, the doorbell rings. "I'll get it," Naomi offers, since Adan's hands are covered in the batter for the fried chicken. "Come on in," she says to their guests, and Lily and Paul walk in with their usual charisma.

"Oh, Adan dear, that smells wonderful!" Lily gasps. "Anything I can do to help?"

"Not a thing, just make yourself comfortable," Adan says.

"Don't mind if I do." She sits down in the living room.

"How is Adan doing this mighty fine evening?" Paul asks.

"I'm good. How is Paul? I'd shake your hand, but—," he answers and shrugs his shoulders to reveal batter-covered hands.

"I'm doing well too, and no worries," he says as he squeezes Adan's shoulder, then joins his wife in the living room. Both have their attention turned to the kitchen, where Adan and Naomi continue to prepare dinner.

After a few minutes of small talk, Adan serves in large plates and bowls the home-cooked traditional meal of fried chicken, mashed potatoes, gravy, and sauteed green beans with bacon. To bring even more Southern nostalgia with it, Naomi serves sweet, iced tea and lemonade. Once the table is entirely filled with food, they all dig in.

"So, you've chosen a date; what about a venue?" Paul inquires just before taking a mouthful of potatoes. "By the way, this food is top-notch," he adds.

"Thanks." Adan laughs. He looks at Naomi then says, "Well, my family has an old hay barn that Naomi fell in love with. We're both leaning toward having it there."

"Oh, Lily, it's so beautiful; you'll love it! It's rustic and set along an open field of golden grass with a big blue pond," Naomi says dreamily.

"Sounds perfect, honey," Lily agrees.

"Where did you two get married?" Naomi quizzes.

Lily takes this question proudly. "In a cave, at its mouth, which was colossal."

"You're kidding!" Naomi gasps. Adan waits to hear more.

"Nope, we had many people there, all packed together. A stream running through the cave echoed and made it hard to hear, but even still, it was something beyond special. We will never forget what it was like standing there and feeling the coolness of the cave wash over us as. All the people we loved were lined up and standing wherever they could find a foothold." She looks like she is dreaming as she falls back in time to tell them the story of their wedding.

"How extraordinary," Adan says, captivated.

Adan and Naomi have a small agenda tied to inviting them over for dinner for the evening, and it is to ask a particular question of Paul. "So, Paul," Adan starts. "We want to ask you something important to both of us."

"Absolutely."

"Will you marry us?"

Paul drops his chicken leg, wipes his hands on a napkin, clears his throat, and says with a bright smile, "I would consider it an honor to marry such fine people as yourselves."

Adan and Naomi give each other a look of glee. "Thank you so much. You have no idea how much this means to us," Adan says.

"You're more than welcome." The four continue in conversation, mostly discussing and complimenting Adan's otherworldly cooking abilities.

Once they are finished eating, Paul says, "Lily and I have a couple of questions. We don't want an answer but want to give you something to think about."

"Okay," they both say as Adan finishes gathering the dinnerware and placing it in the sink. He brings cinnamon rolls to the table for everyone before sitting back down.

"Finances. Decided how you're going to manage them together?"

"Actually, we haven't given that much thought yet." Naomi shoots Adan a nervous glare.

"Also, children?" Paul continues. "You can make that decision anytime, but make sure you're *both* ready *before* having them. Don't feel pressure to have kids soon, either; enjoy life while you're young."

"Definitely." They both nod their heads.

"Finally, Head of Household? Adan, you are the man, so you naturally assume the role of protector and defender."

"Naomi," Lily starts in now, "You are the woman, so you are the comforter and nurturer of the home."

Paul resumes. "Together, you are the Head of Household. Don't push duties off onto one another but be responsible for your part. Work as a team in everything you do. Be honest and sincere with each other, even when it might be uncomfortable. And do not be afraid to ask for help if you are struggling; there is no shame in that. These are the issues that Lily and I have worked through, and they will undoubtedly present themselves to you as well. Think about them now so that they don't surprise you later."

"Wow, thank you so much. We hadn't given it that much thought."

"No need to thank me," Paul says, looking at Lily. "We know you two will live exceptionally well with each other, but we wanted to save you some potential heartache that will come your way."

After thanking them again, Adan's phone rings. "Excuse me," he says, standing up from the table to answer it, leaving Naomi with Paul and Lily at the table. He learns his dad is calling when he picks up the phone. "Hello."

"Adan. Meet me at the emergency room; your mom has been in an accident. She is in an ambulance on her way here now," David says with a solemn but fearful voice.

Adan's stomach drops from under him, and he has to support himself against a wall in the hallway. "Is she okay?" Adan asks, shaking.

David hesitates. "I don't know."

"I'll be right there." Adan finishes and hangs up the phone. He walks back into the room, intently focused on not falling apart. "I have to go to the ER. Mom's been in an accident."

Naomi jumps up. "Is she okay?"

"Nobody knows yet."

"I'll go with you."

"You don't have to. Stay here and keep Paul and Lily company."

"Nonsense." Lily stands up. "We will clean the dishes for you and lock the door on our way out. You both go."

"You don't have to— "

"It wasn't an offer; now go." Lily's voice deepens with authority.

Adan quickly puts his shoes on, Naomi does the same, and they run out the door and into the truck. They drive fast to the hospital, less than ten minutes away. Along the short drive there, neither say a word until Adan cracks under the weight of anxiety. He aggressively wipes his eyes, trying to clear them of tears with no luck.

"I hope she is okay," he blurts out.

Naomi leans over onto him and massages his shoulder and chest. "She will be. She will be." "I don't know what I would do without her," Adan forces through the lump in his throat. He holds his hand on his forehead, peeling his eyes open in rebellion against his tears to see the road in front of them.

"Don't worry about that. Your imagination goes crazy in situations like this, but just focus on making it there, not the worst-case scenario," Naomi comforts.

Although Adan says nothing, he is grateful for Naomi's presence.

The drive from Naomi's house to the ER is only a few minutes, but it feels like hours to Adan. They pull into the hospital parking lot to find David's truck already there; Grandma and Grandpa are there, too. Adan parks and bursts out of the vehicle. He sprints into the building with Naomi only steps behind. He jogs around a corner and enters the waiting room to find his family all sitting together. Just seeing them all brings him a semblance of peace.

"You made it." His dad stands up to greet them.

Out of breath, Adan asks, "Is she here yet?"

"No."

Panic has still not left him. "Do you have *any* updates?"

David shakes his head. "Have a seat; all we can do is wait."

Reluctantly, he sits down next to his grandpa on his right and Naomi on his left. *At least we are all here together. Seeing us all will make Mom feel better If she is hurt.* Even thinking of it as a possibility that Renee is injured makes Adan nauseous. He runs into the bathroom to vomit.

Five more minutes pass by, each more agonizing than the last. "How did you know about the accident?" Adan asks his dad.

"Uncle Alden saw her car and the ambulance leaving the scene."

"Did he say what it looked like?"

"No."

"God, knowing nothing is making this so much worse," he complains and throws his head back, covering his face with his hands. Tears begin to fill his Grandma Esme's eyes; she has said nothing since Adan has been there with them. He is sure she is praying ceaselessly, which inspires him to do the same.

They wait for a painstaking five more minutes until finally, Ashby shouts and points to the ambulance at the stoplight about to pull into the hospital emergency lane. It moves at a snail's pace and has no emergency lights, sending waves of relief through Adan. *It can't be bad if they're not in a hurry.* He smiles at Naomi, who is not yet convinced all is well.

When the ambulance parks, an older gentleman, whom Adan recognizes as Collin Right, exits out of the passenger side and walks inside the hospital. Adan is familiar with most of the faces in the ER, as his mom has worked here as a nurse his entire growing-up. He waves at Collin but gets no response as he heads straight to the nurses' station.

Collin says something inaudible from a distance, and lip reading is useless since his head is at an angle. All three nurses disappear as Collin walks back to the ambulance.

"Why is it taking so long for her to come out?" he asks the air.

As soon as the words fall from his mouth, time stands still; his heartbeat is all he can hear. Everything is motionless except for Collin, who, pulls a rolling bed from out behind the ambulance; on it is a black body bag. Adan's heart rips apart, his knees give out, and he crumbles to the floor, feeling nothing except the tearing of his vocal cords as he screams.

The five days after his mother died passed by slowly. As if nature mourned her passing too, the rain pours and drenches the Ozarks, setting record rainfall numbers for September. Adan hasn't left his bed except to use the restroom, and he hasn't spoken to anyone. Naomi has called and texted multiple times, but he feels no conviction to respond. He assumes his dad and Ashby are doing the same; he hasn't heard anything from them, nor his grandparents. He could listen through the house walls when his dad called Odell to tell him what happened. He doesn't even know if Odell has come home or is staying in Bolivar until the funeral, which he expects to take place in the coming days.

Neighbors and all of Renee's co-workers have brought the Caddell household enough casseroles and desserts to feed an entire army camp, but it all sits untouched in the fridge. Letters and gifts pile up on the front porch each day; David brings them inside but has no desire to open any of them. Ashby spends most of his time in his room and fills it watching TV, which distracts him. Adan is crippled by his pain and heartache; he hasn't even talked to his Abba once since Renee passed away. Sleep does not come to him as he lies in bed—no matter how often he watches porn and mastur-bates—only a self-destructive imagination convinces him over and over again that she suffered immense pain and cried out for help that came too late. He is glad the drunk driver who hit her head-on died, too.

She was driving south of town a few miles to deliver an apple pie she had made for an old friend who had just lost a parent. The road is curvy with no shoulder to speak of, so she had no room to move out of the drunk driver's path. The paramedics explained to the grief-stricken family that she was not awake, but in a coma when they arrived at the scene, then passed away on the drive to the hospital.

David's face showed immense sadness and anger at himself for not being there to protect her, to have comforted her. Adan was crumpled to the floor with Naomi bent over him, caressing his head. Grandma fell against Grandpa, and they wept together. Ashby stood and cried, very much confused and alone. The family's lifeline was taken away. Nobody knew where to begin picking up the pieces of their shattered hearts.

TWELVE

I t's the Saturday before Renee's funeral, and Adan is still curled up in bed, lifeless. He hasn't eaten in 11 days. His dad has tried multiple times to engage with him, but each attempt ends in failure. Ashby has spent most of the last week hanging out with his friends, and David felt it is exceptionally good for him to do so right now to keep his mind busy. Odell and Amira have come down, both taking a leave of absence from work for two weeks. Just as David's attempts to help Adan fail, so do Odell's.

"Man, you need to talk. Just say something," Odell begs his brother. Adan only stays still and silent. His emotions have festered and calloused over, turning him into a stone. "If you don't talk, you'll never make it through this."

I don't want to make it through this.

Odell attempts to bring Adan out from under his blanket of silence, but his words fall flat. "I'm leaving you now, but someone is here to see you."

At this, he rolls over to see Odell disappearing through the bedroom door, but then the beautiful dark face he loves so much comes into view. *Naomi!*

"Hey," she says quietly.

"Hey," he sits up and rubs his eyes. He has lost the top layer of muscle from his whole body, and his natural suntan is gone, leaving him looking weak and pale as a vampire.

Naomi gazes at him with disappointment and sadness in her eyes. "Can I sit?" She points to the edge of his bed.

"Yeah, of course." He moves his feet under the comforter so she can sit down comfortably. "It stinks in here." She crinkles her nose and face.

"Sorry."

"You haven't returned my calls or texts."

"I'm sorry."

"We haven't talked in almost two weeks."

"I'm sorry, Naomi."

Naomi strengthens her posture and sharpens her tone. "Stop saying you're sorry and talk to me."

"I can't." He gives up.

"You can."

"What do you want me to do? Act like everything is okay?" His face distorts into an ugly mess as he loses his composure and sobs. "I don't have a mom anymore."

Naomi sheds compassionate and authentic tears of her own now as she tries to comfort him. "You don't have to pretend everything is okay. It's okay to cry and feel the overwhelming pain you're feeling, but you *must* talk to me."

"I don't really want to, though. I wish I would just die." Saying it out loud now makes him realize how selfish it is, but he honestly doesn't care.

"You don't mean that."

"Yes, I do."

"No, you don't."

"You don't know how I feel!" Adan yells at Naomi, immediately regretting it, but before he can apologize, she slams her hand on the bed.

"I know exactly how you feel, Adan." She glares at him with her powerful eyes. "I lost my brother, and it was my fault," she says through her tears. "I wanted to go to the stupid pool, so I begged that he take me. I've had to live with that choice since I was a nine-year-old girl."

"It's not your fault, Naomi," he says, wanting to comfort her but emotionally unable.

"I try to believe that, but it doesn't help. I know the immense pain of loss, the desire it puts in you to die yourself. But I know you don't mean that because I know you love me." Her voice does not waver but remains strong.

"I feel so alone. I don't want to accept it for what it is. I can't live without *her*."

"You aren't alone, Adan. Not even close."

"Then why do I feel like I am? Why can everyone else accept it, but I can't?"

"There is no denying that your relationship with your mom was special. But consider that your brothers lost their mom, too. Your dad lost the love of his life." She pauses to let it settle on him. "Your grandparents lost their daughter. I lost my future mother-in-law, whom I already adored and loved more than you know. You are not alone in your pain, Adan."

He cries more tears and doesn't know where they are coming from or how his body can still produce them after he has already cried enough to fill the Pacific Ocean to overflowing. "I never even considered your pain. I'm so sorry."

"It's okay," she says as she wipes away her remaining tears. "Pain has a way of separating you, making you feel as though you're alone in the battle against it. But it is simply not true. I'm here for you; your family is here for you."

"I still don't think I can do it."

"Do what?"

"Live."

"Look me in the eyes." She faces him, taking up his full view, and he can almost get lost in the river of blue and green of her eyes. Supporting herself with her arm on his leg as she leans over, she says. "Keep taking breaths. That is step one. Two, keep loving me."

He can't help but smile at Naomi's simple analogy. "I can do that."

She smiles back at him. "Then that's it, baby, you'll live." He can laugh with her for a short moment; it stretches and expands his lungs, giving him a rush of energy.

"You know, she prayed I would find and marry someone like you," he tells her. She says nothing, only listening for more. "She wanted me to have someone I could talk to and be honest with." He scratches his head nervously. "I need to tell you something."

"Okay." She scoots closer to him and rubs her hand along his legs.

"Ever since she has been gone, I've watched porn and masturbated too many times for me to count." Somehow, he finds the courage to keep looking her in the eyes. "It used to be something that plagued me as an addiction, but through Abba and you, I overcame it. But now..." He finally looks away from her. "Now it's back with a vengeance. It's the only way I can distract my mind, if only for a moment. I'm so sorry," he says with a crack in his voice.

"That's okay, Adan. Porn is something I know many people struggle with. I'm sure this is only a temporary setback, a natural part of grief. Don't let it destroy you; you'll get past it, and we will together."

Adan casts her a confused look. *How is she so cool with this?* "Are you sure?"

"Totally. You aren't the first or only person to struggle with such a thing."

"Wow," he says with realization. "I've lived half my life thinking I was unique and alone in my addiction."

"Sounds like addiction and pain work in many of the same ways." *She is right. Addiction causes pain, and pain fuels addiction.* "They work together to create a vicious cycle."

"Yeah, vicious, and stinky. Let me help you take a shower," Naomi adds.

His head and eyes perk up. "Okay." She peels the covers out from over him, and he slides out of bed in a yellow-stained white shirt and boxers.

"You're so cute," she chuckles.

"You really think so?" He looks down at himself.

"With your messy hair, yeah, I think so."

He smiles more than he has in what feels like forever, which gives his cheeks and jaw a much-needed stretch. He points Naomi to the location of his clothes drawer, and she picks out clean socks and underwear, then a nice shirt and jeans from his closet, and follows him into the bathroom.

Each step hurts. His muscles haven't had to stand for more than just a few moments at a time until now. She makes him undress in front of her so she can help him in the shower. While he is in the shower, she takes his dirty clothes, along with his bedding, to the laundry room and adds a generous amount of extra soap to the washer.

While standing in the shower, he soaks up the hot water like a sponge. He can feel the blood flow and the color of his skin returning to him. His breath deepens in the humidity, and his vocal cords sing in gratitude. When he thinks of his mom, in a split-second thought, he remembers what Naomi said. He repeats to himself many times, "Just breathe. I love Naomi." When he is finished in the shower and opens the curtain, he finds Naomi standing there waiting to help him dry off and put fresh clothes on. "Thank you."

"You're welcome," she says. With the new energy and Naomi's presence, he can't help but get caught up in the moment. He takes the towel from her hands, wraps it around himself, pulls her near him, and gently kisses her with increasing passion. She gives in to him, putting her hands on his chest to feel his heartbeat, and he lifts her onto the counter.

Kissing her neck, he whispers, "I love you."

"I love you too," she says, nearly out of breath. He starts to pull her shirt off, but she stops him. "Not now." She swallows. "Someone is going to be here any minute."

"Who?"

"You'll find out soon enough," she says as she drops off the counter and runs her hand along the top of his towel, causing it to drop to the floor.

"Hey." He smirks.

"Oops," she says as she walks out of the bathroom.

After buttoning the last button on the top of his shirt, the door-bell rings. "I'll get it," Naomi offers, leaving Adan standing in the middle of his room.

"Who is it?"

"You'll like who it is, don't worry," she says over her shoulder as she leads the way out of his bedroom into the living room. David, Odell, and Ashby are nowhere to be found.

"Where is everyone?" Adan asks.

"They left for the evening to give you and me some breathing room."

"Oh, okay," he says. It's the first time he has been anywhere but his bed and bathroom, and the moment he sees the couch and his mom's favorite cushion, a dam inside him threatens to burst. *Just breathe; I love Naomi.*

As soon as she opens the door, Paul's wise and kind face appears through the doorway. He carries a posture of overflowing empathy. He walks up to Adan, squeezes his shoulder, and grasps him tightly, not saying a word.

Lily follows Paul in, and after hugging Naomi and crying, she wisps gracefully over to Adan and, with her signature hug, sweeps him up along with the absorbing aroma of her perfume. Real flow-ers. "I love you, Adan. We are here for you. You don't have to try to do this alone anymore."

He nods his head and wipes the small tears from his eyes. "I've missed you too."

"We've missed you even more," Paul says, and Lily nods in agreement.

"I brought dinner." Lily lifts a picnic basket into the air. He hadn't noticed her carrying it until just now. "Shall we eat?"

"Yes, I'm starving!" Adan says excitedly. *I haven't eaten in over a week.*

All four of them head into the kitchen, Lily leads the way, and Naomi brings up the back. Again, at the sight of the kitchen and the smell of Lily's food, the dam inside him quivers. *Just breathe. I love Naomi.*

Adan indulges in the food Lily brings but is careful to not stuff himself entirely, as it is common knowledge that eating after a fast can shock the digestive system. They make simple dinner-time conversations. Paul, Lily, and Naomi are careful to not bring up any subject that could lead to Renee. After a little more than half an hour, though, Paul asks, "So this is the first time you've been out of bed in the last week?"

"Yeah," he answers.

"I'm glad you chose to do so; it's good to see you and hear you speak."

Adan simply nods his head and smiles. He already knows Paul is here to make certain he is okay. Sitting on the bench beside him, Lily begins to rub his back. "Honey, we know how much you love your Momma. And I know how bad it hurts, but I also know how much worse it is to process it alone. We are here for you, day or night."

He realizes now that Naomi and Lily have talked about him, because their advice and support overlap. He finds it sweet coming from them, whereas if it were anyone else, he would be angry that they used him as a discussion topic. "Thank you."

"You don't have to thank us, that's what friends are for."

"I know." He smiles.

Naomi stands up from the table. "I'm going to call it a night." She moves her attention to Adan. "I'll put your sheets in the dryer, but it's up to you to put them back on the bed," she says with kindness beaming in her eyes.

"Why are you leaving?"

"Going to my parents to visit for a little while."

He can tell there is more to the story but doesn't press her for more. "Okay. Love you."

"Love you too; see you tomorrow." She finishes with hugs for everyone then leaves the room. The look on Paul's face answers the question of Adan's as to why Naomi left. *He wants to talk.*

"The funeral is in less than 72 hours now; Lily and I will be there and right beside you if you want us to be."

The thought of the funeral sends waves of nausea over him. What is the purpose of an event where people just come up to you and feel sorry for you? "I don't think I can be there," he says sharply.

"I know how hard even just the thought is to carry. This is something you need to be at, not for you, but for everyone who loves your mom and family."

"It's going to be too hard." Tears well up in his eyes.

"That is why we're going to be there, along with your whole family and Naomi too." *Why does everyone keep talking to me like I'm a child, especially now?*

"What if I don't want to go? Is someone going to make me?" he asks, letting the question hang in the air.

"No. It is up to you to be there. It's entirely your choice," Paul admits.

"Thank you." He relaxes.

"The reason I even bring it up now is that your family wants you to speak."

"What?" he gasps.

"They weren't sure how to ask you, so they asked me if I could run it by you."

"You expect me to speak at my mom's funeral? How could I even stand up at such a thing?"

"I expect nothing from you, and neither does anyone else; it's only something they *wanted*," Paul clarifies.

"I've spent the last 11 days in bed, practically willing myself to die. Then, Naomi comes here—which now I see was with agenda—and made me feel that I was capable of life still, that I had a reason to live, but now I wish I were dead again." Heat rises in him as his anger grows at no one in particular, just the situation. The last thing on earth he wants to do is have to talk about his mom in front of a crowd of people. *No way!*

"Naomi came here with no agenda except to see the person she loves. Same as why we are here. We love you and are expecting nothing," Paul explains carefully.

"Okay." He relaxes again.

"Have you talked to Abba?"

Anger fills him immediately again at the question, except this time, it is directed entirely upon one person, God Himself.

"How could I talk to the one who took my mom away from my family and me?" he asks with an angry voice.

"He loves…"

Not even waiting for Paul to respond, he continues. "He put her through a horrific and painful accident. He let someone else's stupid choices kill her." His breath shortens, and his lungs begin to burn.

"You don't think it hurts Abba too? You don't think He is feeling the same pain you are now?"

"Why would I care how He feels? He obviously takes pleasure in people's suffering."

"That is not the case, Adan." Paul shakes his head but keeps his kind eyes focused on him.

"How could it not be? Look at all the pain and suffering occurring worldwide every day. He created that, lets life continue, and does nothing about it."

"He did do something about it," Paul counters.

"What?"

"Jesus."

"How does saving us from our sins, but not the wickedness of life, help? He literally just expects us to suffer through this life until we die, clinging to the hope of spending eternal life with Him—the one who caused all the horrors of the world in the first place."

"Adan." Paul shuffles his chair, leans forward, and places his elbows on the table. "God is not in control."

Adan gives a purposefully confused glare at Paul. "That makes no sense whatsoever."

"Of course, he has all power and all control, but he gave us free will. This means he can control all things, but he chooses not to. This is the only way free will can exist. God is not the one who caused your mom to drive on a specific highway; it was her choice. He also isn't the one who caused that driver to drink enough to intoxicate himself, then get into a truck and drive. It was his choice."

"But He could have stopped him from driving, though. He could have kept the whole situation from happening, but He didn't."

"Yes, there are many things God could take control of and make better, perfect even. But again, he offers us free will. He doesn't, however, promise a life free of consequences, good or bad. That is life. We make our choices and face the consequences. Jesus came so that we could be rescued from eternal hell. He reconciled us to himself so that now we can have a relationship with Him and know Him personally. We know where our eternity lies. This life has terrible moments, but we can fully enjoy the good ones, knowing that this isn't our home."

"But I am angry at God. I trusted him."

"Anger is a natural part of grief. It's okay; you don't have to deny it. Share it with Abba, though. He isn't afraid of your anger. He can bear your doubting and your questions. He wants to comfort you with his spirit and help you heal."

"It's Naomi who will help me heal. Not God," he corrects.

"In a lot of ways, Naomi will help you heal, but God is the only one to bring you to complete healing. He has to be who you depend on, even more so than Naomi. You'll need to depend on Him for everything, your very breath, through the processing of this grief, and for all things. Depending on Naomi for your healing and life will become too much of a burden for her. Humans were made to help each other, but not fulfill each other. Only God can satisfy your soul and heal your mind. Let *Him* be your everything."

Adan sits still and looks blankly into the space between him and Paul. He knows he is right. It isn't fair to Naomi to put so much pressure on her. But so much of him absolutely loathes Abba now. He can't stand the thought of Him just standing by and allowing such a tragedy. Letting his mom have to suffer unfairly, even for a moment. Abba couldn't possibly know what it is like, or he would take control and make things good and right. *Except He did stand by and watch his own son be beaten and tortured to death.* "God obviously has no problem allowing the ones he loves to suffer, though. He just looked down from above as His son was killed."

"Jesus chose to die on the cross. To succumb to the traditions of man, so that we could be reconciled to Himself."

"God could have stopped it."

"Adan, Jesus is God. Our God chose to die for you and me because he loves us."

"Oh." Letting Paul's answer settle in his mind, he sits back in his chair. "I'm sorry, Paul, for how rude I've been to you this evening. I'm not angry at you, just angry at God and the circumstances."

Lily reaches her arm over him and says, "You don't have to apologize, dear. It's good to cry and ask the questions on your heart. Grief has no definition except that of tremendous pain. Be kind to yourself; you have a long journey ahead of you."

"Thank you, Lily," Adan says.

"We will get out of here now; we don't want to be too much of an intrusion."

"You are more than welcome here; in no way are you a bother."

"That's sweet of you," Lily says as she packs up her food and tosses the paper plates they used into the trash. Before they leave the house, both Paul and Lily give Adan a hug. "Don't stress about the funeral; nobody will blame you if you choose not to speak," Paul says.

"Thank you," he finishes, and they say their farewells for the evening.

Adan drives over to his grandparents' home, and just as he suspected, his whole family is there. Well, almost the entire family. This will be the first time he has spoken or even looked at them in what feels like forever. His Dad notices him first when he walks through the doorway and stands to greet him. Neither says a word but only embraces each other for a moment. The same applies to everyone he hugs in the room. When he finally greets his grandma, he can see the mysterious green eyes in her, the same as his mom's. "Love you, Grandma."

"I love you too," she says with the softest tone.

He takes a moment to find his seat before confronting all the eyes still trained on him. *They expect I must have something to say.* "I'm sorry I abandoned all of you. I was caught up in only how much I hurt and had no regard for your pain of equal magnitude. I love you, and I am here to stay now." He speaks clearly and with conviction. His heart really is sorry, and so his words come out authentically.

His dad responds first. "Don't apologize. We all grieve differently." Odell repeats his dad's words, and so does Grandpa.

Grandma Esme, however, has some of her own to offer. "You have such a special relationship with your mom; your absence was justified. But oh, how glad I am to see you again."

"I'm glad to see you too, but there is no way I can speak at the funeral." Adan doesn't hesitate to make that a clear point.

David responds. "That is okay. Nobody wants you to feel like you have to. We all just know how good of a speaker you are." *Yeah right.*

"Good. Thank you."

"But think about it until Tuesday," Grandma Esme adds. "You could change your mind."

"Doubtful," he reaffirms. She just smiles back with her comforting and sincere charm.

The family visits for over an hour before Adan heads home, with David and Ashby following just behind. The conversation lacked something; they all knew what it was, and would have to get used to their gatherings never being the same.

Sunday, September 15th

Good morning, Abba. I hate you.

Monday, September 16th

Good morning, Abba. I'm sorry I said I hate you. After thinking about it all day yesterday, I realized I'm still angry with you. I trusted you, and my life was good. I had a whole and wonderful family, and I was soon to be married to Naomi, whom I love, then you just allowed my mom to be taken away from us. It's not fair, Abba! I don't understand how you can love me and still put me through so much pain. I didn't even get to say goodbye to her. I have spent the last year devoted to you. I thought I knew you well; I've spent many mornings with you. It was hard at first, but then it became easier. Eventually, it was my favorite part of the day; right now, though, the only reason I am here is that I want closure and to be able to say I am done with you from here on out. I can love you when life is good, but if life is this terrible, then—. *What am I saying?*

Oh, Abba, I am so sorry. I am so, so sorry. I've only ever known what it is like to have a relationship with you when my life is the same day in and day out. I've never had to experience pain like this before. I'm sorry for blaming the accident on you; I know it wasn't your doing. I'm sorry I abandoned you and the rest of my family. I've missed you so much, and I'm sick from all the anger I have pent up. I love you; I really do. I love you more than anything, Abba. I need you; I need you more than ever before. I've only known what it is to love you when life is good, but now I need to know what it is to love you even when life is awful. I can't do this alone, not even for one more day. Thank you for my family and my friends. I'm sorry for forgetting how blessed I still am.

I can't believe I ever considered not coming to you. I wish you had just taken control and forced me to come to you sooner, but then it wouldn't be love at that point. My heart is broken and will be for a long time, but you give me hope, life, and joy.

THIRTEEN

T he day of Renee's funeral arrives. It will be held at the family's church. The funeral home is expecting over 500 people in all to attend the service in support of her family. When anybody asks Odell why he is making the funeral such an enormous event, his answer is always, "Mom was not an ordinary person, so it only makes sense to have her service be extraordinary."

Adan has truly been encouraged and inspired by Odell's conviction to put this event together. He has coordinated county-wide to make sure it goes smoothly. Amira has put in an equal amount of time and support. She has managed to help countless out-of-state family and friends coordinate their flights and hotel arrangements. David and Esme have shown their support of Odell's efforts, helping in any way they can. Ashby has been a helpful hand to both Odell and Amira, running errands for them without a single complaint. It is only Adan who doesn't participate. His goal is to simply survive it.

Adan and Naomi have spent the last two days together, keeping each other company. He hasn't told anyone except her that he has decided to speak at his mom's funeral. He told her only because she was in charge of aligning the speakers and band, a job which she gladly offered to do for Odell. Otherwise, he wouldn't have told anyone that he was speaking.

"I have you speaking last," Naomi says as she reviews her agenda sheet.

"The words everyone will remember," he says.

"Absolutely, because your words will be beautiful."

"No, I meant because people always remember the last thing said at events. The same goes for endings of books, speeches, and songs, whether good or bad," he corrects her with a roll of his eyes.

"That's true, but *you* will do an amazing job."

"You're too kind," he says sarcastically. "Who is first?"

"Your preacher is going first, then Doctor Martinez, then you."

"So, three in all. That isn't many people to entertain such a huge crowd."

"They aren't coming to be entertained."

"I guess that's true."

"After you speak, your church's worship band will sing a couple of songs."

"Oh, that's nice. They will make sure everyone gets a good cry," he says.

Grandma is cooking breakfast for everyone to help start on a positive note. "Come eat, you two," Esme says to Adan and Naomi.

"Be right there," Adan yells.

"Guess we are done here." Naomi shoves her clipboard to the edge of the coffee table.

Grandpa, David, Ashby, Odell, and Amira sit in the dining room, and Grandma pulls the biscuits out of the oven.

They eat their breakfast in silence, and when Adan and Naomi join them, only hand gestures are used for greeting.

Finally, Odell breaks the silence with a question. "You're okay with being a pallbearer, right?" he asks Adan, who nods. "I'll need your help after eating; Ashby and I still have a few chairs to set up."

"I'll be there. It's about time I help with something," Adan says.

"Perfect, thanks."

Sitting in the presence of his family is a vital comfort. Even though they lack one now, the power of family remains true. Family, along with Abba, is the only reason he can walk and the only reason he will be able to survive the rest of the day. The impending emotional hurricane that awaits him later today looms dark and heavy over him, but Naomi's smile beaming in his direction is like the sunshine pushing away the shadows. He reaches into her lap, grabs hold of her hand, and mouths the words, "I love you."

At the church, which is in the direct center of town, Odell, Ashby, and Adan unfold and set up about 100 chairs along the center aisle of the sanctuary. The stage faces 500 seats, and when standing on it, it gives the impression of standing amidst a vast arena.

The service starts at 6 p.m., but all the family is there by 4 p.m. to finish any other tasks that need to be completed before people start arriving.

"It's really looking beautiful in here now," Naomi says as she admires the many bouquets of flowers placed eloquently throughout the aisles and chairs and in front of the stage.

"It really does," Adan admits and thanks the small team from the flower shop as they leave.

He's surprised that he can see beauty at such an event as this.

The funeral home arrives at 5 p.m. sharp, and Adan, his brothers, Dad, and Grandpa each carry the casket holding Renee, place it at the front of the stage, and surround it with all the freshly delivered flowers. Thankfully, his mom always made it clear to everyone that she despised open caskets, so it was unanimously agreed to close her casket lid.

Just as the casket is placed in its spot, the first guests arrive, sign in, and find a seat. The following guests are none other than angels from heaven.

"Paul and Lily!" Adan shouts, as he rushes to them to give each a hug.

"We made it," Lily says in return, with her luxuriously comforting smile that Paul possesses too. "Where would you like us to sit?"

"I have a couple seats reserved for you." He leads them to the row reserved for family and offers each a water bottle.

"Thank you," they say with gratitude, their thanks exaggerated by the end of summer heat still in the air.

As the 5:00 o'clock hour goes by, Adan continues to greet guests as they arrive and help them find a seat. Something about keeping busy helps him not panic over what he will say in the minutes to come. He has nothing written down and not even a plan for what to say except a short poem he wrote about his mom. Every time he sat down to write something, he would be flooded out by his tears.

If that is any indication as to how I will react when trying to speak on stage, then I'm likely going faint from both sadness and embarrassment.

Over 400 people have now arrived at six p.m., and there is still a line of people needing to find a seat. It takes 15 more minutes for everyone to be seated and for the service to start. Just as Naomi planned, Adan's family's longtime Pastor Canvey walks onto the stage and begins with an introduction and predictable prayer. He has been the Caddell family's pastor for over twenty years, and his preaching had easily influenced Adan's image of God growing up. Canvey does an exceptional job of keeping the crowd's attention for the time speaks.

After Canvey finishes his nearly 25-minute speech, Dr. Martinez, a longtime coworker and friend of Renee and her family, graces the stage. This man is humble yet confident in the way he presents himself. He tells three short stories about Renee, all revealing her profound impact on the people around her. "For me, Renee was an example of what real love is. If she showed that even to me, it's no wonder when I look at her family here today, I see her love exuding from each one of them," he says as he looks at the row of heartbroken people. He finishes his time speaking on a strong note of hope and encouragement for everyone in attendance. After he is done, almost everyone claps with a heart of gratitude for the returned smile on their faces.

Until this moment, Adan had ignored the bile rising in his throat, but now he must swallow it and make his way to the stage. His jaw is clenched to keep from shaking under the immense pressure he has set for himself. The stage remains empty as it awaits Adan's presence. *Get up.*

You can do this.

"Don't forget to breathe," Naomi whispers in his ear.

He stands up from his chair, takes one long and deep inhale, and maneuvers across his row of family, releasing breath with each step. He notices people mumbling and whispering along his way to the stage. He hears each footstep like the pounding of thunder. When he finally makes it to the stage's stairs, his legs weigh more than steel and make climbing the steps an enormous challenge. He turns to face the crowd with the microphone at his mouth.

Abba, help me.

Words, from out of nowhere, completely unplanned, come pouring out of his mouth. "I have always been at an advantage in life. I've never known what it is to not be loved. My mom made sure of that. It's easy to take that advantage for granted. The part of this that has proved most difficult for me is that I didn't tell her 'thank you' enough; more than that, I didn't say I love you enough. I want desperately to go back in time and give her a thousand more 'I love yous'.

"She poured her heart and soul into everything she did; my brothers and I were no exception.

I have learned over the last few days—although it will take the rest of my life to implement— that mom is far from gone. She lived not for herself but for others. She is alive in the love our family has for each other. She is alive in the wonder and awe I experience when watching a sunrise or sunset. She is alive in my love for my future wife, Naomi. Her energy and spontaneity are a part of Odell, Ashby, and Dad. She lives on *through us.*" So far into the speech, he has been powered entirely by endorphins, but the weight and reality begin flooding him, and his voice catches. He pauses a moment to swallow and take a few deep breaths.

Once he can relax in his lungs and throat, he continues. "She taught me how to see the good in the small things of life and nurtured it in me. With time I grew up and began overlooking many of those small parts of life, but she never did. Everyone here was impacted by her in some way, and I'm sure could also testify to this: she made you feel *seen* and *highly regarded.* I've always felt like somebody special after talking to her. She lived in a world full of beautiful people. Taking what I have learned from her, I intend to do the same from here on out.

"I wanted my mom to be at my wedding. As any son would, I thought she would be there so we could dance together. More than anyone else, she wanted to see me happily married and fulfilled, but now she won't ever be able to see that." He stops to wipe away his tears. "I won't let that bring me down; I am, however, a little jealous of Jesus now, because I know she's got herself wrapped around Him, and they are dancing to her favorite 1980s music." The crowd laughs at this through their tears.

"Today is hard; tomorrow will be, too, and the day after that. But we can't let our pain cripple us; we must continue walking in love and kindness. We all know that is what she would want. Besides, she is with Jesus, and her Father, the ones she loves the most; for her, there is nothing but joy. I have wondered how I could possibly continue to carry on without her, a part of me has deemed it impossible, but I remind myself that she has a lasting influence on my life forever. It is by relationship that we will make it through. Relationship with our families, our friends." He waits to speak again, looking out at the row of people who hold such a profound place in his heart. Grandpa, Grandma, Odell, Amira, Ashby, David, Paul, Lily, and Naomi.

"But the relationship that will truly carry me through is the one I have with God, my Abba. He is the one I love more than anyone or anything. Our relationship grows sweeter every day. He is the one I blamed for my mother's passing, but that is far from true; I see that now, yet He remained with me as I accused Him of it. He didn't force his love on me; He only reminded me of it and allowed me to return to it. His love was present the whole time, even if I denied it. The more love I have for Abba, the more love I have for my family and friends and for everyone around me. I love each of you here today; you have no idea how much your presence means to our family.

"I'll leave you with this; it is a simple poem or note that I wrote about Mom, whichever you want to call it. "Like the wind that blows through mountains and valleys, stirring the leaves of mighty trees and the petals of a million wildflowers, her voice speaks. Both with fierceness and authority but equally soft and sweet. Her heartbeat pulses like ocean waves, and her mind works in harmony with the network of all nature. Her eyes are more vivid than a sea of green. Her face is more elegant than all the flowers on the earth. Her hands care and nurture three, never wavering. As it is human nature, our bodies must die, but our spirit lives on. The three she raised up can carry on her legacy of love; now, though, she can learn to fly. She can dance and be embraced fully by her father, the one who stitched her together in her mother's womb. This was never her home, or anyone's for that matter. This is only a temporary moment in our eternal lives, the rest of which Mom can now enjoy.""

Immediately after finishing, he leaves the stage and sits beside Naomi again. The crowd applauds for a few moments until the church worship group fills the stage. They lead the crowd of 500 into an a cappella rendition of "It Is Well with My Soul." The power and magnificence found in a body of people singing in harmony eliminate all distractions and fill the heart to overflowing. Adan lets his tears fall, this time without any attempt to withhold them. *Tears feel so good when you don't try and hold them back.* He doesn't have to look around to know that everyone else is crying too. The song lasts for an easy ten minutes, and nobody wants the singing to end.

The instrumentalists now begin playing soft ambient tones as the crowd steps forward one by one to give their condolences to the family. Many of the guests Adan has already greeted, but still finds it a pleasure to embrace them all. He is surprised to see his uncle Alden in the last remaining crowd funneling through.

"Love you, boy," he says gruffly. "You did a fine job speaking up there."

"Thank you, Uncle Alden," Adan replies. "Love you too." Thankfully he continues down the row of the family since Adan has no idea what to talk to him about.

Paul and Lily bring up the end of the line. "Thank you so much for being here," he tells them both.

"Absolutely. And you spoke with an authenticity today that your mom would be so proud of," Lily says.

"Thank you," he replies, and they continue on to each member of his family.

They weren't the last ones in line like Adan had thought; Lisa and her husband followed.

"Hi, Lisa!" Adan says excitedly.

"Hey, Adan. You did a truly wonderful job this evening. I want you to know that I was one of the people your mom made feel like somebody important. She's the reason I had the boldness to find someone who loves me," she says, glancing at her husband and smiling, "and to go after my dreams of owning a restaurant. She was a special lady. If you ever need anything, you call me. You understand?"

"Yes, ma'am," he says with a smile, and she hugs him.

It is 9:00 o'clock by the time everyone leaves the church. Adan looks around and sees the hundreds of chairs still unfolded throughout. "Do we have to put these up tonight?" he asks anybody who is listening.

"Nah, we can do it tomorrow," Odell says.

"Perfect. I am tired."

"Me too," everyone says in unison.

"Sweetie, you did a wonderful job tonight. You should be proud," Grandma says to Adan and kisses him on the cheek.

"Thank you, Grandma."

"I'm glad you decided to say something. I knew you were the one who needed to speak," David says, patting him on the back. Everyone mumbles in agreement.

"Thank you for that, but I have had enough attention for one night; let's go home."

"Yes. Let's go," Ashby says, and everyone agrees, tired and ready for sleep.

That night, Adan stays with Naomi since the day was too full for him to have given her much attention. He is trying to make up for the time they lost together because of his selfish grieving. Naomi assures him it is fine, but he can't shake the feeling that it is something he must do.

"I'll sleep on the couch," he says as they walk into her house.

"Really?" She gives him a confused glance.

"Yes."

"Want some water?"

"Yes, please. I'm parched."

"Me too."

He heads to the restroom, and when he comes back into the living room, Naomi is sitting on the couch holding two glasses of water, waiting for him.

"Thank you!" he says before he sits down and chugs the entire glass. "That was good."

"Good; hope you still feel good after your stomach starts cramping," she says with a serious face. He only smiles back at her, caught up in her warm glow. He sits the cup down on the coffee table, then moves onto her cushion and wraps his arm around her, pulling her in as close as possible.

"You are the most beautiful person in the world," he says softly.

"You are too sweet, a little unoriginal, but I'll still take it," she smiles, and he knows she blushes beneath her gorgeous black cheeks.

"Okay, give me a minute and I'll come up with something original," he offers.

"No need. It'll just be corny; stick with what you know," she says, then he drops his head to place a small kiss on her lips. "That is exactly what I meant."

"I figured."

Her smile fades away, replaced with a more purposeful expression. "I want to ask you something," she says.

"Okay, good or bad?" he asks worriedly and straightens his back.

Ignoring his question, she says, "You love Abba more than anything. Does that include me?"

Oh my gosh, how do I answer this? "Yes."

She takes a moment to respond. "Why?"

He moves forward to the edge of the couch, then turns his body to face her. "Naomi, I love Abba with all my heart, and the love only grows with each passing day. Because I love Him more than anything, it allows me to love you far more than I could if I didn't love God with greater measure. For me, Abba has become my everything; I am still learning, but I know this, I was born, everyone was, with a clear purpose, to love, and be loved by Him."

Naomi has tears streaming from her face now. "I'm so sorry, Adan."

"For what? You don't have to be sorry for anything." He kisses her forehead.

"I don't love God like you do, so I'll never be able to love you as well as you love me."

"Oh no, please don't worry about that. I respect your position with God, as does God."

"But still, it's not fair to you."

"I'm not worried about fair. Our love for each other is good; that is all that matters."

"I wish I loved God like you do."

"Oh gosh, no. Don't look at me as an example; I am still a work in progress. Just up until yesterday, I was at complete odds with Abba," he says, pausing for a moment. "So, you do love God?"

"I don't know. Maybe."

"You do believe in God?"

"Yes."

"How well do you know Him?"

"Compared to how you talk about Him, we're complete strangers."

"No, don't compare your relationship with God to mine. They may look worlds different." He shakes his head. "In fact, they most likely would."

"I've just always believed and was taught that if I believed in Jesus, and went to church, then I am good to go. But I don't really believe that anymore. I know there is more than that now, but it feels unnatural."

Adan smiles and huffs lightly. *I know exactly how that feels.* "Talking to an empty space, attempting to engage with someone you can't see and doesn't speak in words is not normal, and it is okay to feel awkward. Humanity has grown apart from Abba ever since Adam and Eve.

Turning ourselves back to Him is not going to be quick and easy, and trust me, it's going to feel unnatural."

"But you get past that part, right? Why am I still feeling this way?"

"Yes, absolutely. It took over a month for me to finally feel comfortable with Him, and we would spend every morning together, even on weekends. A year later, I'm still learning new aspects of His presence; I'll never fully understand Him and His mystery, but now I am comfortable in His presence, and He reveals Himself to me in His own timing. I also used to *tell* Him I loved Him; now, though, I truly mean it." He waits for his words to settle on her ears before answering her question's second part. "What are you doing to try and know God better?"

"I pray."

"When did you start?"

"The night we got engaged," she answers softly.

Adan's heart melts inside his chest. *How could she possibly think she couldn't love me back in equal measure?*

"That's not even been a month."

"Well, getting to know Him shouldn't take this long."

"How often do you pray?"

"When I go to bed at night."

"Do you fall asleep in the middle of your prayer?" he presses.

She cranes her neck to give him a look of confusion. "How did you know that?"

"It's pretty common."

"Now I feel stupid." She throws her head back and rolls her eyes.

"Don't! You're not stupid. That is how *most* people pray."

"Whatever."

"Let me ask you, how well do you think we would know each other if we only ever talked right before you fell asleep, and our conversations were usually left unfinished?"

"Not very good, obviously."

"How can you expect anything different of God then?"

"Then what do I do? How do I not fall asleep when I'm talking to Him. I'm the one putting in all the effort."

"For one, I choose to visit with Him in the mornings, and two, I journal while we make conversation. It typically lasts an hour to two hours."

"An entire hour!" Her jaw drops. "How do you have that much to say?"

He laughs at her surprise. "Again, this is just me, but my relationship with Abba is intimate and good. We can talk to each other for an hour or more and always have more to say the next day. And when He and I aren't talking to each other, all I can think about is sitting down and visiting with Him. Though He is present with me all day, there is something extra special about having time together completely focused on one another."

"See, I want that," she says, slapping her hand on the armrest of the sofa.

"I think you want immediately what has taken Abba and me over a year to have." He remembers how he felt over a year ago, the same as Naomi is feeling now.

"Wait here; I have something." Adan has continued purchasing Daily Kairos journals, as they last only thirteen weeks, and he still has a new one in the truck. He runs out, grabs the package, and runs back inside. "Here you go."

"What is this?" She demands.

"That is the same journal that helped guide me into my relationship with Abba. Of course, along with Paul and Lily's support, but you have me for the support!"

"I suck at journaling."

"Oh, me too. Really bad, but this is simple, trust me."

"Should I start it now? You can help me."

"No. Conversation with God is intimate and private. Find a quiet place, don't have your phone nearby, and just follow the journal prompts. Then, like we are now, we can discuss it together."

"Okay," she says, trusting him.

"Please only do this for *you* because you *want* to, not because you think you *have* to for *me*."

"No. I really want this for me. Hearing you talk about your relationship with Him over the past year has inspired me, but I do want this for me. I'm tired of being angry at God," she says.

Adan pulls her onto himself and lays down on the couch. "You and I both!" With her head resting on his stomach, he massages her shoulders. "It's going to be a process, believe me, but you can do it; I'll walk beside you, and before you know it, Abba will be the love of your life." He can feel her neck muscles flex to form a smile. "By the way," he says, "I can't wait to be your husband."

"You're the best," she says. He stops massaging, waiting. "You want me to say it too?" "You're kind of leaving me hanging." He laughs.

"Adan?"

"What?"

"I can't wait to be your wife."

FOURTEEN

The month of December arrives faster than usual this year; considering all the anticipation for the wedding; it is not a surprise for Adan or Naomi. They have spent the last two weeks at his family barn, cleaning it out and preparing it as the place for the small wedding ceremony. The decorations Naomi has picked out are modest and small. Lights are strung overhead, and each century-old wood beam holds a white and purple mixed flower bouquet. Adan's only decoration responsibilities are to hang the bouquets, and he is grateful for the simple duties she gave him.

Naomi chose to simplify her wedding decorating even more than initially planned because she wanted daily massages added to their honeymoon package. "14 days of full-body massages or a more cluttered wedding ceremony? It's a no-brainer," she said to Adan the day they sat down to book the trip.

However, Lily has taken it upon herself to add a dash of natural beauty to the barn using bouquets of herbs from her garden. Not only does the lavender and lemon grass add character, but it also helps to clear the barn smell out and replace it with a fresh and clean aroma that is far more inviting. She supports Naomi in her pursuit of a simple wedding but can't help but add some of her unique sparkles to it, which is gladly welcomed by Naomi and Adan.

Naomi's Mom, Rachel, has also helped with some other minor details, but Naomi was sure to make it clear that it was *her* wedding, not her mom's. Even a simple wedding such as this can cause tension between the bride and her mother. To honor her mother, though, Naomi will be wearing her wedding dress.

Grandma Esme has been a steady support for both Adan and Naomi, offering advice only when asked. She and Naomi have bonded exceptionally well over the past few months, and she has put multiple stamps of approval over her for Adan, as any grandma would feel the need to do.

David, Odell, and Ashby will be Adan's best men, and with Paul officiating the wedding, he couldn't be surrounded by more people he loves.

It is Friday, the day before the wedding, and Naomi and Adan are desperately trying to decide on a playlist but are doing a better job of arguing than making any kind of decision. "Naomi, we cannot have country music playing; people's ears will curl up and die." Adan attacks her favorite music genre.

"You're such a baby. We're getting married in an old barn; it screams the need for country music," she counters.

"I'm not a baby," he defends himself. "Why don't we do half and half?"

"We can't mix pop and country; it will confuse people."

"Seriously?" He gives her a sarcastic side glare.

"Fine. But I'm walking down the aisle to the song I want," she demands.

"What song? Do I even want to know?" He cringes.

"You'll find out when I come walking down the aisle."

"Then I get to choose the song we walk out to."

"Deal. Those are the two most important; the rest my brother can choose."

"Agreed."

"You better leave now, it's getting late, and I need a good night's sleep for tomorrow."

"You're kicking me out?"

"Yeah. Go."

"Welcome to your new life, Adan," he says to see her reaction.

"That is a positive attitude," she says with a laugh.

Before leaving, he takes their cups from the living room and puts them into the dishwasher. "Okay then, I guess the next time I see you, you'll be dressed in white."

"I guess so." She walks up to him and wraps her arms around his waist. "I love you," she says softly, expecting a kiss.

He denies her and returns, "I love you too," giving her only a quick kiss on the cheek. She glares at him.

"Why did you just avoid my lips?"

"We have our whole lives left to spend with each other and only one day remaining to enjoy the anticipation; I just wanted to add to it." Before the last word is entirely spoken from his mouth, she pulls his head down and kisses him passionately.

"Hey!" He smiles like an excited kid.

"Don't avoid *these* again." She looks at him with fire in her eyes, pointing to her beautiful, full lips, then turns around and walks away.

"Understood." He laughs on his way out.

David, Odell, and Ashby are waiting for him at his house. "What are you all doing still up?"

"Just want to ensure we have everything done for tomorrow," Odell says.

"I really think so. Tables and chairs being set up was the biggest part."

"And that is done," Ashby says proudly.

"Are you ready?" Odell asks.

Adan sits down on the sofa before answering. "Yeah, it still doesn't feel real, though."

"I know how you feel there."

Adan doesn't really like talking to Odell about his wedding. He becomes jealous, not because it was so extravagant, but because Renee was a part of it. Adan doesn't have that luxury. "I love her so much; that's all that matters."

"That is exactly right. You'll always be nervous about something this big, but it will also always feel right," David says with a crack in his voice caused by an onslaught of memories.

"Thank you guys so much for your help getting all this ready."

"Not a problem. It was simple, and we're glad to do it for you," Odell says, and David and Ashby nod their heads in agreement.

"Love you all; I'm going to bed," he says, exhausted from the day of anticipation.

"Goodnight. Sleep well; you have a big day tomorrow," David says. A restless sleep awaits, considering the amount of expectancy flowing through him.

Feels like I am waiting for Santa to come on Christmas Eve.

He wakes up a couple hours earlier than usual, especially for a Saturday. In December, it stays dark in the morning until after 7 a.m., so he finds himself at his chair and desk visiting with his Abba. When the sun finally begins its crawl up the horizon, he sees the sunrise, which draws him outside onto the patio to watch it. "You never cease to blow my mind with every sunrise, Abba." Something about this morning is especially peaceful as the sky brightens magnificently before him. The rays gently expose the silhouettes of the trees. Fog fills the valley in front of his house, adding mystery.

He is reminded of how beautiful his mom was. "Tell Mommy I said I love her." He stands still and lets his tears fall for the loss of his mom, but no longer are they tears of pain and confusion, only longing and hope. He can hear the patio door open and close behind him; he turns to see who it is, but already knows it is his dad. David walks up next to Adan with a cup of coffee in hand.

"It sure is a beautiful morning, isn't it?"

"Absolutely."

"It reminds me of your mom. Because it's beautiful, but also because sunrises and sets always fascinated her. Our first date included time for her to watch the sunset before dinner," he says, smiling at the sun. "Most things remind me of her, though." He is crying now too. Adan puts his arm around his dad's shoulder, and they both shed their own tears. *Today is going to be an emotional day.*

The day moves quickly, with 4 p.m. only a few minutes away. Lily and Grandma Esme have prepared a delicious full-course meal for everyone at the reception. They have now found their seats in the front row. Lily is wearing a homemade dress made of plain, natural fabric, yet she is easily the most noticeable person in the crowd. Grandma Esme is wearing a baby-blue dress that compliments her eyes, drawing attention to herself as well.

There are fewer than 30 people in attendance, making it feel all the more intimate and memorable for everyone there. The barn smells lovely with all the lavender and lemon grass Lily has scattered throughout.

Adan and Paul are already at the altar, with David, Odell, and Ashby. Naomi's mom and two of her dearest friends stand on the opposite side. Everything is as it should be, but Adan still feels unable to be fully present. *I wish Mom was here; she would love this so much.*

He continues in distracted thought until suddenly, the conversations die away when Naomi's father comes into view at the barn entrance, awaiting his daughter. One of her brothers, serving as DJ, selects a song from his phone. "From This Moment" by Shania Twain. Immediately when the music begins, Naomi walks up to her father, then he takes her arm in his. Seeing her burns away all distractions, pulling Adan entirely into the present moment, reminding him exactly why he is here. *She is literally glowing.*

Once the song's chorus starts, they begin walking down the aisle toward the altar. Adan doesn't even feel his tears trickling from his eyes as he gazes at her. Her dress is forever long, sweeping up the attention of everyone as she walks, and it compliments every curve of her body.

Finally, when they make it to the front, and her dad gives her away, Adan whispers. "I actually liked that song."

She is crying too, but it doesn't keep her from smiling at him. "I knew you would."

The music dies away, and Paul starts, saying, "What a blessing it is to witness and be a part of two beautiful people's marriage." Everyone voices their agreement. "I've known Adan and Naomi for a little over a year now, but feel as though I've known them forever, Lily and I have such a strong love for each of them. Their hearts are devoted to one another, but more than each other, to God. They do not boast, but only in their faith and relationship with God. I have witnessed their growth and development over the last year, and I have learned much from watching them."

Paul turns his attention to Adan, then to Naomi. "It is an honor to know each of you. You hold a special place in both my and Lily's hearts." His attention returns to the small crowd. "That is enough of my rambling; each will present their vows. Adan."

Usually, he would be nervous about speaking in front of a crowd, no matter the size, but standing next to the woman he is about to spend the rest of his life with, he has complete confidence. "Naomi. I have spent so much time trying to figure out what the perfect words are to say, but finally, I realized that no amount of words, no matter how eloquent, could ever convey how much I love you. So today, I marry you, and I will spend the rest of my life attempting to show you how much I love you."

"Naomi," Paul says.

"Adan," she blurts, wiping her eyes so she can focus. "I've had a crush on you since the first day I started working as a receptionist at the law office." She smiles, showing off her dimples full scale. "I thought you were hot, but when we started talking, I discovered that you were the most interesting and emotionally intelligent man I'd ever met. After that, you became irresistible to me." The crowd and Adan laugh. She visibly holds back a flood of tears.

"When I look at us now, both ready to commit ourselves to one another, I see how much we've both grown. You've helped me heal from the pain I've had since I was a little girl. I've watched as you've had to go through a tremendous amount of pain too. This life isn't fair, but by the grace of Jesus, we found each other. I am convinced that together we can make it through anything. I love you, Adan."

Paul wastes no time. "By the power vested in me, I pronounce you husband and wife. You may kiss the bride," he says with excitement.

After they kiss and solidify their marriage, they walk through the aisle to the barn entrance to the song "Happy" by Pharrell Williams.

While walking, Naomi looks at him. "Happy?"

"I am!"

"This is a perfect song!" She sings. Both smiles so brightly that the lights hanging above cannot compete.

Where the barn held the wedding service only moments ago, it has now transformed into a reception gathering with the aroma of first-class, Lily-style food being served. The barn's dirt floor provides a quality dance floor for Adan and Naomi. They both move to the slow rhythm of the music, caught up in the bliss of their new commitment and expression of love.

When Naomi's father, Ralph, is done eating, he asks for Naomi's hand, and they slowly dance to the song "I Loved Her First." I knew she would pick that song to play at some point. Adan leans over to tell Paul, who is standing beside him.

"It's a good one."

"It definitely is." He smiles.

"Thank you again, Paul. It means the world to both of us that you married us."

"No, thank you for allowing me to. You and Naomi are beautiful people and are a beacon of hope for your generation. I am so glad I could be a part of it." Having no idea what to say back, he just gives Paul a firm handshake and hug.

Naomi and Ralph's song ends after a few minutes, and Adan quickly finds his grandma. "You ready to dance, Grandma?"

"You bet! But not to none of this slow music; let's do something fast!" she yells out.

"You got it." Adan waves at Naomi's brother running the music. "Something fast," he tells him.

He throws a thumbs up, and immediately the song "Footloose" starts playing. *Oh no!*

"That's what I'm talking about!" Grandma shouts.

Three minutes of intensely embarrassing dancing for Adan later, the small crowd shouts and claps for the spontaneous entertainment provided by him and Esme.

"You did great, Grandma."

"Thanks, but you could use some practice, honey," she smirks, then hugs him.

"Wow, you're just mean." She ignores him, finds Grandpa, and they begin dancing together slowly, as do Paul and Lily, Naomi's parents, and Odell and Amira.

David and Ashby and Naomi's brothers are the only ones not dancing. Naomi looks at David, then back to Adan. "I should dance with your dad for a minute. He is left out."

He looks at her and says, "That is a great idea." She and Adan walk back to the side of the dance floor, and she takes David's arm and lets him lead her to dance.

Adan watches beside his little brother. Ashby has a small trail of tears running down his cheeks. "You okay?"

He nods his head. "Yeah, I just wish Dad could be dancing with Mom."

"Me too. But we all still have each other; that'll be all that matters in this screwed-up world."

"I guess so. I'm glad I have my friends too."

"For sure. We're gonna make it through; it's by the people we love that we will." Ashby nods his head again as he continues watching everyone dancing.

Adan looks at them too. Smiles fill the room, joy exuding from everyone. *This is the perfect wedding.* His heart struggles to find complete happiness without his mom, but he sees his grandparents together, holding each other up. They can still smile after losing their only daughter.

He sees Odell and Amira, his best friend happy with his wife, who is expecting a baby soon. They even plan on naming their little girl Renee.

He moves his attention to Paul and Lily, two people that came into his life and turned it upside down. *Turns out life is better that way.* If it weren't for them, he might still be trapped in his selfish, self-loathing mindset. Now, though, he is free and in a relationship with his first love, Abba.

Naomi and his dad move back into view now too. David is laughing and smiling as he dances with his new daughter. He lost the love of his life, but he will soon have a granddaughter; in addition to his children, he still has much to live for. He returns his attention to his brother again. "I love you, Ashby; I'm always here if you need me."

"Thank you. Love you too," he says, and they embrace each other.

Everyone eats their fill for another hour and dances as their heart desires. When the evening reaches 9:00 o'clock, most people are packing their belongings and calling it a night. When it is just Adan, Naomi, Odell, and Amira left, they sit at an empty table. Paul and Lily packed all the food and dishes, leaving the tables clear.

"We have some exciting news!" Odell says through a huge grin.

"What is it?" Adan asks like an expectant child.

"Well…"

"You better tell us quick; neither of us is a fan of surprises," Naomi says, and everyone laughs.

"I've talked to the school board here in Mountain View, and the head football coach is retiring in the Spring." *I think I know where this is going!* "We're moving back next summer!"

Adan is filled with so much happiness at the thought of having his best friend back where he can see him every day that he could easily faint. But instead, he jumps up from the chair and shouts. "You have no idea how happy I am right now!"

"You're giving us a pretty good indication right now," Amira says as she embraces him too.

"We are happy about it too," Odell offers.

"I've found a possible job at the clinic in town. I'm taking a year off to care for little Renee, so I have plenty of time to find a job," Amira adds.

"That is excellent," Naomi says. "I can't wait to be able to see my little niece every day!"

"I don't know if it's from getting married, finding out you're moving back home, or that we leave for Tahiti at 6 a.m. tomorrow, but I am beyond excited but also exhausted," Adan admits. "All the above," Odell laughs. "You two get out of here; we will put everything up tomorrow; you won't have to worry about a thing."

"Thank you so much," Naomi says graciously. "You're the best; love you both," Adan adds. "No problem, see you in two weeks!"

On the short car ride home to their house, Naomi says, "This dress is pretty, but I can't wait to get out of it."

"Me either," Adan says, then blushes. "I mean out of this suit," he corrects, then pauses.

"You're exhausted, and we have to wake up early tomorrow, but you're not *too* tired, right?" She asks.

He turns his head toward her slowly and dramatically, and with the most serious face and voice he can muster, he says, "Oh, definitely not."

FIFTEEN

He is awakened softly by the gently rolling waves lapping at the edge of the small hut, floating over the unbelievably turquoise water. The warm ocean breeze flows through the room, bringing to life the white curtains covering the open windows. Naomi is still fast asleep, so Adan takes this moment to his advantage to go on a short hike.

There are no clocks in Tahiti, and they have tucked their phones away in a drawer, agreeing to not let them be any kind of distraction. *The best memories are those when you are fully present in the moment, soaking up the image that will last a lifetime.* Before he rolls out of bed, he carefully kisses Naomi's forehead. He quietly changes into a t-shirt and shorts, decides to go barefoot to add to the experience, and is sure to grab his journal and pen too.

He leaves their cabin just in time to catch the last few minutes of the sunrise. Purple, pink, and orange flaunt their irresistible splendor, captured effortlessly by the clouds floating in their midst. *Now that is the definition of gorgeous.* He walks along the wooden walkway with water on both sides until he reaches the island. This morning he chooses a small hiking trail, only one mile long. He and Naomi have already been on it, but he remembers the perfect place to sit, beside a waterfall overlooking the ocean.

As he walks, his feet sink into the ancient volcanic soil, rich with nutrients to support the luxuriously thick plant life all over the island. It is both soft and grounding. Once he makes it a mile up a low-grade hill, he comes to the small waterfall and is alone. *Perfect.* He situates himself upon a moss-covered rock, hanging effortlessly over the small lagoon where a waterfall flows. He sits back on the rock, hears the waterfall humming, and looks out across the ocean below.

> Good morning, Abba. I love you so much. I know I was here just yesterday, but I still can't get over the incredible view it is from up here. You took your time when crafting the islands of Tahiti. Thank you so much for my beautiful bride, Naomi; she is so dear to me and is a constant reminder of your goodness. I can't help but wonder where I would be right now without you. Certainly not here.

> Abba, my life is far from perfect; you know my struggles, pain, and doubts. But, I have learned something incredible about my life: the people in it. My family, You, and my friends. It doesn't matter what job I have, where I live, or how much money or stuff I have, but what makes this life worth living is the beautiful people surrounding me in it. I still get down about losing Mom, but you pick me up. I still

struggle with porn at random, triggered moments, but your grace is sufficient and strengthens me. I still despise myself some days and feel like I'm not good enough for Naomi, and certainly not you, but you remind me I am a good creation. I can't imagine my life without you because it no longer exists. I will live in a world full of beautiful people. If only a year and a half of knowing you, and I already know you this well, I can't wait to spend the rest of my life with you!

After penning the last few words, he closes the journal and rests in the melodic sounds of nature all around him. He is so in tune with the soundscape that he doesn't hear the footsteps drawing closer behind him, moving swiftly and silently; then, when upon him, Naomi yells and grasps his torso. He immediately jumps away from her in fear and adrenaline but lands directly in the center of the lagoon under the waterfall. He comes up from the water, gasping for air, but hears no apology from Naomi, only a full-bodied roar of laughter. He quickly swims to the edge of the water, and before she can realize he is coming for her, he picks her up in his arms and carries her up on the rock he was just sitting on. He lifts her over the edge of the rock, and she screams, "Don't drop me in. She wraps her arms around his neck, begging for mercy.

"You don't have to be scared."

"Then don't drop me in; I'm so sorry; I won't do that again." She laughs nervously, still clinging to him.

"Too late for that," he laughs.

"Please don't!" she squeaks.

"I'm not going to drop you."

"Oh, thank you." She relaxes.

Before she can realize what is about to happen, he says, "We're going to jump together!" Adan leaps from the rock, with Naomi in his arms, and together they crash into the azure blue water.

The End.

ABOUT THE AUTHOR

BRITIAN BELL is an artist passionate about loving people, song-writing, storytelling, and inspiring a better world.